Quentin

Quentin

BOURBON & BLOOD
Book Four

CHASITY BOWLIN

Quentin
Paperback Edition
Copyright © 2025 by Chasity Bowlin

Love N. Books Press
An Imprint of Wolfpack Publishing
1707 E. Diana Street
Tampa, FL 33610

www.lovenbookspress.com

Cover design by Jennilynn Wyer Designs
Edited by My Brother's Editor

Quentin was originally self-published in 2024 by Chasity Bowlin.

Paperback ISBN 979-8-89567-749-0
Ebook ISBN 979-8-89567-748-3
LCCN 2025946309

Quentin

One

Quentin eased out of his car in the parking lot of The Kicking Mule. It was the only bar within thirty miles of Fontaine, and it only existed because a sliver of Woodford County butted up against the main road into town. Kentucky's blue laws were notorious for making the sale of alcohol tricky. Location, time of day, day of the week, and even holidays could make something as simple as buying a drink nearly impossible.

It was the very definition of a dive bar—sawdust on the floor, a chain-link fence around the stage, and glass crunching underfoot with every step. But he needed a drink, and he needed it to be somewhere his family wasn't. He felt raw, rocked to the core. It was more than just the ass whooping he'd gotten. It was his mother.

Being in that house, being reminded of every horrible thing that had happened in their lives was just too much to bear. It was the cowardly thing to do, running from it the way he did. But he wasn't like Mia or Clayton. He'd accepted that he didn't have the same kind of steel inside him that they did. Every time he looked at Patricia, he just wanted to lash out, but the person his anger was directed at was never there. Samuel was long gone now, hopefully for good. So, he'd gone for the next best thing...the stranger among them.

His newly discovered half brother had been on the receiving end of Quentin's bad temper. He just hadn't been prepared for how little of it his half brother would be inclined to tolerate.

When punches are thrown before Thanksgiving dinner is even served, you *know* it's a bad day. Holding his ribs, hoping they were just bruised and not broken, Quentin limped toward the door of the bar. He was too damned old to get into fights like that. The truth was, even if he'd been younger, stronger, and in a hell of a lot better shape, Ciaran Darcy would still have handed him his ass. He'd been outclassed, outmaneuvered, and had written checks with his big mouth that his body couldn't cash.

Judging from the number of cars in the parking lot, the crowd was light. It wasn't surprising. Even hardcore drunks would spend the holiday with their families. Quentin stepped through the open door into the darkened interior and moved toward the bar. There might have been five people in the whole place, including him and the bartender.

"I'm getting ready to close up," the bartender said, tossing the words over her shoulder without looking in his direction.

He looked her over, soaking in every detail from head to toe. Her hair was lighter. She sported a shade of blonde that had never been found in nature. It was shorter too, just barely brushing her shoulders. Memories stirred in him, of her kneeling on the bed, her long hair wrapped around his fist as he sank into the heat of her. The odds of that ever being repeated were about as good as the odds of him suddenly developing the ability to kick Ciaran Darcy's ass. In other words, next to never. "I know you are," he finally said. "I'm very familiar with your schedule."

She did turn then. Her brown eyes, so dark they were almost black, were shooting daggers in his direction. "We're already closed to you."

Harlow Tate had every reason to hate him. He'd dicked her around, bailed on her, kept her at arm's length, and generally been a gigantic, raging ass. The fact that she hadn't pulled out the shotgun she kept under the bar was a miracle. She had a hell of a temper and even better aim. Of course, even having her throw shit at him was a better option than quiet civility. If Lowey got to the point where she could just be polite to him, then any shot he'd had with her would truly be long gone.

There was only one way to answer that question. He had to poke the bear. "That's not what the sign says," he replied, jerking his head in the direction of the blinking neon near the front door.

She frowned then. "What happened to your face? I thought I was the only one who hated you that much."

A smile started but quickly morphed into a wince as it pulled his split lip. "I have a gift for pissing people off."

"Especially women," she said. "But I don't think a woman did that much damage to you unless she outsourced."

"A family matter...uh, disagreement," he explained, easing himself onto one of the barstools ever so carefully. Fuck, his whole body hurt. And it was only going to get worse. Ciaran could throw a punch like a goddamn hammer. "You think maybe I could get a drink?"

3

"You think if I give you one, you'll get the hell out of my bar and never darken my door again?" she shot back. Even as she asked the question, she'd pulled a bottle of bourbon off the shelf and was filling a glass for him. It was not Fire Creek. She reserved that for people she liked.

If he said it, he'd stick to it, and that was a promise he wasn't willing to keep. Evading the questions he didn't want to answer was more his specialty. "I can't make any promises."

Lowey set the bottle down with a thud and pushed the glass toward him. "That's the most honest thing you've ever said."

"I never lied to you, Lowey. Not even to tell you the things you wanted to hear," he stated softly before he took a sip of his whiskey. It burned like hell. It didn't even deserve to be called rotgut. "Son of a *bitch*."

Her gaze raked over him coldly enough that he felt a chill in its wake. "I'd say that's just about right...you've had your drink. It's time for you to go."

"Lowey—"

"Don't call me that," she said stiffly. "That name is reserved for friends, family...for lovers. You don't fit into any of those categories. Not anymore."

"I did once," he reminded her gently. And it had been fucking amazing. Nothing in his life had ever felt as good as being with her, and that right there was the heart of the problem. He'd left her because he was afraid he'd come to need her too much. The hell of it was, all he'd done was prove himself right.

She glared at him as she wiped the bar down far more vigorously than necessary. "And if it had meant so goddamn much to you, then you wouldn't have walked out on me the way you did. Leave, Quentin. It's what you're good at."

4

Quentin placed the glass back on the bar. There was nothing he could say to her that would change anything he'd done, and there was nothing she'd said to him or accused him of that wasn't true. Part of him wanted to cut and run, to chalk it up as a mistake and cut his losses, but that was the kind of thinking that put him in his current situation to begin with. He had to show her he'd stick. He had to make her see that he wasn't just playing her. And that meant taking whatever lumps she threw his way.

He let his gaze rake over her again, committing every curve to memory, every luscious inch of her. Seeing her up close and in person, remembering the texture of her skin, the sweet scent of her hair, and the way she felt beneath him...there wasn't a word in existence that could describe how much of a fuck-up that was.

"I'll go, Lowey...but this isn't over. This thing between us was too good, and I'm not going to give up on getting another shot at it."

"And if wishes were horses, Quentin Darcy, beggars would ride. It'll be a cold day in hell!"

He smiled at her. "Guess I need to dig out my winter clothes then, don't I?"

As Quentin turned to leave, the window imploded. Flying glass hurled through the air at them. It was instinct more than anything that had him diving over the bar, taking her to the ground with him. It was fear that kept him there, shielding her body with his own, as the sound of gunfire filled the bar.

Glass shattered above them, sharp pieces of broken bottles and the mirrored shelving behind the bar rained down on them. His clothes took the brunt, but a few of the larger pieces weren't so easily deflected. Even with him to shield her, Lowey hadn't escaped without injury. He could see blood on her hands from the glass on the floor and minor nicks and cuts.

"Son of a damn bitch," he hissed. "What the hell is going on?"

She glared up at him. "You tell me! They didn't start shooting until you walked in! Who the hell else have you pissed off, Quentin?"

"Nobody who'd want to put in a bullet in me!" he snapped. Well, except for his father, but that wasn't really Samuel's style. Even if it was, he'd never do the dirty work himself, and right now he was too damned broke to hire anyone.

When the last of the gunfire faded, the quiet was overwhelming. It was broken by the sound of an engine revving and the spewing of gravel in the parking lot. Quentin stood up and raced toward the door, what was left of it. It cost him. Every bruised muscle, every abused inch of him protested. But he managed to get a look at the ancient beat-up truck and the lack of a license plate. It didn't matter. He knew exactly whose truck that was.

Turning back to the bar, he saw Lowey staring around in dismay at the wreck of her business. "Don't guess the sheriff bothered to inform you that his cousin—your ex-husband—was getting out of jail, did he?"

Her face paled considerably, but her lips firmed into a hard line and the look in her eyes would have withered a lesser man. "No. That asshole didn't tell me."

Quentin nodded, then looked back at the two old drunks who were still sitting on the floor under broken tables. Neither of them appeared injured. In fact, they were grinning from ear to ear at the excitement, prompting him to shake his head.

"Call 9-1-1, report the shooting."

She laughed bitterly. "They won't do anything! Hell, he almost killed me and barely served a year!"

"No. They won't arrest him. They won't stop him. But if you don't file a report, then your insurance company won't pay for the damages...and I don't think you're ready to tackle that out of pocket," he explained.

She sat down then. Heavily, as if the weight of the world was suddenly pressing down on her. "I hate this. I should just leave. I should just sell what's left of this place and go."

He couldn't tell her no. The truth was that she was right. Getting the hell out of Fontaine was the best thing Lowey could do, for herself and for him. But those words wouldn't come. So instead, he said simply, "This is your home, Lowey. And you're too damn stubborn to give it up."

A bitter laugh escaped her. "You're right about that. You'll have to call the cops...they won't show up if I do it."

Quentin sighed and pulled his cell phone from his pocket. He didn't question her statement at all. The entire family that she'd had the great misfortune to marry into at the tender age of eighteen was full of rednecks and assholes, the two descriptors not being mutually exclusive. He didn't labor under the illusion that Sheriff Silas Barnes would hurry just because his last name was Darcy.

Two

L owey retreated to the bathroom of the bar. At the back of the building, the restrooms had at least been spared the worst of the damage. Still, a bullet had traveled through the wall and embedded itself in the mirror. The spider web crack around it brought home to her just how much danger they'd been in. Her hands trembled as she tried to shake the bits of glass and wood from her hair.

She had half a dozen tiny, stinging cuts all over her, but Quentin had borne the brunt of it. She still couldn't fathom how he'd moved so quickly given the shape he was in. Someone had kicked his ass up one side and down the other, and while she was feeling somewhat more sympathetic to him than normal at the moment, there wasn't a doubt in her mind that whatever he'd gotten, he'd asked for.

No one, not even her nutball, rage-addict of an ex-husband, could make her as crazy as Quentin Darcy could. And he'd made it more than clear that he wasn't in the market for anything more from her than rolling around in the sheets from time to time. So why was he there? Why, when his life had clearly gone to shit, and she unknowingly needed him the most, did he have to show up? And, of course, he was saying all the right things, too. But then, he was good at that. Quentin could be a charming devil, at least when he was trying to get in your pants, he was.

"Get it together, Lowey," she whispered to herself. "You're going to have to face down your asshole ex-in-laws, and you can't do that if he's mucking up your brain!"

With some degree of composure returned and most of the glass shards shaken out of her clothes and her hair, Lowey walked back into the main room of the bar and felt it all shatter around her again. It had been her grandpa's before it was hers. He'd come back from Korea and opened a little watering hole, as he'd liked to call it—a gathering place for men. Eventually, women had taken up coming there too, but by and large, it had been envisioned by him as a place where other old soldiers like himself could gather. It was a place where they didn't have to worry about being polite or following the rules of a society they didn't really belong in anymore.

Now it was a shambles. The last connection she had to him, and to her grandmother also, had been destroyed. It looked like the war zones he would never speak of to her, or to anybody else. There were things broken and shattered on the floor, pictures and mementos of his life that she would never be able to repair or replace. Joey Barnes had robbed her of something else, she thought bitterly. He hadn't been content with convincing her to marry him when she was still too young to know better, then ruining her life. He'd had to come back and fuck it all up again and again.

9

"You okay?"

Lowey looked up and realized that she'd just been standing in the middle of the room in a pile of broken glass and busted wood, staring around like someone in a trance. The question had come from Quentin, who looked at her with enough concern for her to believe he might actually care. But she knew better than to fall into that trap again. Regardless of what he'd said, he wasn't someone she could ever count on. Sure, he didn't want anything bad to happen to her, but counting on him for more than that would just get her heart broken.

"I'm fine. Just trying to assess the damage," she lied. "You don't have to stick around. I know you've got better things to do with your time than help me deal with the Barnes Family Drama Hour."

"If I leave, I just have to deal with the Darcy Family Drama Hour," he said. "Hell, it might even be a two-hour special after today...besides, I'm the only one who saw Joey's truck. And we both know Silas is going to give you a ton of shit about this. Somehow, he'll make it out to be your fault."

Truer words, she thought bitterly. Whatever else could be said of the Barnes family, they knew how to stick together, through thick, thin, and probation. Silas had given her shit at every opportunity since the day she'd turned Joey in for cooking meth. She'd filed for divorce while he was incarcerated for that, and Silas had written her tickets for everything coming and going. Then Joey had gotten out, beat her half to death, and somehow, by sending him back to prison for it, she was *still* the bad guy.

Thinking about the Barnes family wouldn't get her anywhere. She'd been questioning the family dynamic and how they functioned for years, and it still wasn't any clearer. So, she focused on something else altogether.

Curious and wanting to think about anything besides her ex-husband and his misbegotten clan, she asked, "So what did happen today?"

Quentin had his hands on his hips, the jeans he wore riding low on lean hips with a plaid shirt and a V-neck sweater over it. The shoes he wore probably cost more than her monthly car payment. He'd clearly been in a fight, then he'd rolled around in busted glass and spilled liquor to save her ass, and he still looked like he'd stepped right out of a men's fashion magazine. She hated him for that—more than a little.

"I got into a fight with my brother," he replied evenly.

"You and Clayton? That's hard to believe."

"Not Clayton," he answered. "My *other* brother...the new one."

She wanted to know more, but given what she already knew of Samuel Darcy, she was a little afraid to ask. The Darcy family drama was way more high-end than her own homegrown variety, but that didn't make it any less toxic. The degree of Quentin's inability to commit to anything other than running away from relationships was proof positive of that.

On the surface, Quentin appeared to have it all together. He dressed nicely, drove a nice car, went to work every day, and while he drank more than he should, he never got sloppy. And if the day ever came where he couldn't just drop the bottle without looking back, she knew he'd quit or die trying. Quentin Darcy was too determined to never need anyone or anything to be an addict. But he was still a hot mess on the inside, and that son of a bitch Samuel Darcy was one hundred percent responsible for that. Good Lord, did she really want to go down that road again?

Parts of her said yes. They said it eagerly and with

great enthusiasm. He wasn't the only lover she'd had since her divorce, but he was certainly the best. No one had ever made her feel the way he did or made her feel the same kind of intense need that he did. Recalling just how good it had felt, how dazed and desperate he could make her with nothing more than a touch, Lowey knew that her willpower had no chance of outlasting her need for him. She'd cave. It was just a matter of time.

The thought had no sooner crossed her mind than the sound of approaching sirens filled the bar. Gravel spewed as they flew into the parking lot like a bunch of stunt drivers, or more accurately, like a bunch of overgrown adolescents in cars they didn't have to pay for.

"If they scratched my paint..." he muttered.

Lowey rolled her eyes. He babied his car. She was pretty sure he petted it and called it pretty names when no one was looking. "It's fine. I'm sure your car is fine. If it's not, either your insurance or mine will cover it."

"That's not the damn point, now is it?" he asked.

The door, or what was left of it, flew open with enough force that it banged against the wall. One of the already fragile hinges simply gave way and it listed to one side a little as Sheriff Silas Barnes strutted in. Like the cock of the walk, as her grandmother would have said, she thought bitterly. God, she hated him—him and his whole damn family.

"Looks like you've had a rough day, Lowey. But it's never an easy thing...running a low-rent establishment like this. Especially when it caters to the lowest population in the town," Silas said.

"My patrons did not shoot up my bar, Silas," she snapped. "Your cousin did...the one who is on *parole* and who I was supposed to be notified of his release since he tried to kill me and all."

Silas smiled. "We're behind on paperwork. Budget cuts. Besides, there's no way to say for you to be sure that Joey did this. Why, I just talked to his mama, and he's sitting at home on the couch right now. Been there all day."

Lowey laughed. "His mother who is so cowed by every single bullying man in your family that she wouldn't even sneeze unless one of y'all gave her permission?"

The smile never left Silas's face, but there was a coldness in his gaze that hadn't been there a moment earlier. He was just as cruel and vicious as Joey. He'd just gotten better at covering it up. "I don't like your tone, Mrs. Barnes."

"Tate," she snapped out the correction with a little more heat than was wise when dealing with an officer of the law. More calmly, she continued, "My name is *Ms. Tate*. I took it back the second I shed myself of your worthless cousin...he was here. He shot up my bar. He could have killed any one of us!"

"You've got no proof," Silas said. "I'll be happy to take a statement and write up a report for your insurance company that an unknown assailant allegedly damaged your property."

Quentin wanted to strangle the smug bastard. While he knew that Lowey wanted to handle things on her own, he also knew that because of her history with Barnes, it would never be handled fairly. Silas Barnes was as crooked as a dog's hind leg, to quote Evelyn's favorite phrase. She'd been with the Darcy family for a generation, so clearly, she'd know.

"I saw your cousin's truck driving away, Silas. Cut the bullshit, and go pick his ass up!" he said.

"But did you see my cousin?" Silas shot back.

Silas Barnes was a first-class asshole, Quentin thought. But there was no way to answer that question to their benefit without lying. His fists clenched at his side, Quentin kept his tone cool. "No, only the vehicle. But I imagine it would be easy enough to ask around town and see if anyone else saw Joey driving it in the last half hour or so."

Silas wasn't smiling. He looked like he was choking on something. "Don't you tell me how to do police work, Quentin. The Darcys might have the run of everything else in this town, but they don't own the law...not yet anyway."

Quentin knew better. Samuel had been paying Silas off for a decade, ever since he took office. He'd overlooked, covered up, blatantly ignored, and pinned shit on other people to benefit Samuel for years. But pointing that out wouldn't help Lowey. So Quentin did something he hated more than he hated the bastard in front of him. He swallowed his pride. "Just a thought, Sheriff. No offense meant."

"Well, there was plenty taken," Barnes replied. "Make a list of the damages and get it to me, along with a written statement of what happened. I don't need to tell you that naming a suspect without any proof would not go well for you, do I?"

Lowey sighed. "No. You don't have to tell us anything, Silas. You've made yourself very clear. I'll have the list and the statement to you tomorrow morning."

"You too, Darcy," Silas added. "Being local gentry doesn't get you out of your civic duty." The last was uttered with a smirk and a tip of his hat as Silas turned and headed for what was left of the door.

When the man had left, Quentin looked straight at Lowey and said, "I hate that fucker."

"Yeah, well, find me someone who doesn't."

Quentin shook his head with dismay. "It's an elected position, for fuck's sake. How does he keep winning?"

She looked at him then like he'd grown a second head. "Really? Your daddy is Samuel Darcy, and you have to ask how underhanded shit happens in this town?"

There was no refuting the logic in that. Every dirty deal, rigged election, and plot that had taken place in Fontaine could be practically be traced back to Samuel in one form or other. The man was like a goddamn parasite, a poison vine choking the life out of everything around him. He took root and spread. Deciding to focus on more immediate concerns, Quentin asked, "Where are you staying tonight?"

"Here," she said. "I'm not letting that son of a bitch run me out of my own home."

Her "home" was a tiny little apartment above the bar. Looking up at the holes in the ceiling, he shook his head. "Hell, you don't even know if it's structurally sound! Not to mention, there's no way in hell you're staying here alone so that he can come back and finish the job!"

"If he wanted me dead, I'd be dead," she said. "He's just trying to make me pay for sending him to jail."

He wanted to choke her, or shake her, or do something to make her see reason. Instead, he said the one thing neither of them had ever thought he would utter. "You're coming home with me."

15

Lowey gaped at him for a second before laughing, though there was no mistaking it for a sound of amusement. "Oh no. *Hell* no. I'd rather take my chances with the dumbass I married!"

"Goddammit, Lowey! He could have killed you today! And maybe, as you say, he wouldn't have meant to, maybe scaring you was all he had on his worthless mind, but he's not exactly the sharpest knife in the drawer, is he? Everything that fucker has ever done in his life has gone wrong!"

All of that was true. But going to Quentin's house now, when they were well and truly over, when he'd never seen fit to take her there before, was too much. Every night they'd spent together—no, she corrected. He'd never spent the night with her. He'd always left after he'd gotten what he wanted...well, what *they* wanted. She wasn't going to pretend that she hadn't wanted him, too. Every encounter between them had occurred in her tiny apartment, surrounded by the pink frills and white painted furniture he'd found so amusing.

Not many people had ever seen the softer side of her. They expected her to be the same tough chick who worked the bar every night with a baseball bat and a sawed-off tucked under the counter. He'd thought it was hilarious, calling her little apartment The Dollhouse.

"I'm not going to your house, Quentin. Not now. Not after everything that's happened." Her tone was soft, and her words were perfectly civil, but there was steel in her voice. They both knew she meant it.

"What the hell is your problem, Lowey? I'm trying to keep you safe!"

The fact that he was so infuriatingly oblivious made her want to choke him. "Do you have to ask? Really? I was your little fuck buddy for months and never made it past the front door...and now, because you've crooked your finger, I'm just supposed to go pack my bags?"

He'd never meant to hurt her. Keeping his distance, especially while Samuel was still in town stirring shit up, had been necessary for her protection, but it had also been a convenient excuse to keep her at arm's length. Not that it mattered, she'd still snuck under his skin, and there she was still. She'd gotten in his head and now he had to find a way to get back into hers. "Then we'll go somewhere else, but you're sure as hell not staying here, and you're not staying anywhere alone."

Three

The former carriage house was tucked away behind the two-story brick house with its grand, multi-columned facade. As Quentin guided the car along the curved, tree-lined drive, Lowey noted her surroundings and how supremely out of place she was.

He'd made a series of phone calls while she'd gone upstairs and packed. Quentin playing the hero was a pretty novel concept, not because she thought he was a coward but because she was simply stunned that he'd been moved to care. Or cared enough to be moved to action. She'd fully anticipated that he'd just cut and run again. But no, he'd had to actually come through. And now they were pulling up in front of a house that reminded her in vivid, living color of just how far apart they were.

"You've got a funny idea of laying low," she said. "I was expecting some no-tell motel on the shitty side of Lexington. Not Tara from *Gone with the Wind*."

"They're friends," he said. "And the whole property is secured."

The gate alone was worth more than all her worldly

goods. "Well, if my asshole ex-husband shoots it up, I sure as hell won't be able to cover the damage."

She felt the weight of his stare as he looked over at her. Assessing, curious, and oddly sympathetic, it pissed her off on principle. "What?" she demanded. "What is it now?"

He shrugged, "I could tell you that you're just as good as anyone else, but it'll only piss you off more."

The fact that he was right didn't soothe her already ruffled feathers. "I always knew we were from two different worlds, Quentin, but my friends only come to houses like this one when they've been hired to clean them."

The car eased to a stop in front of the ivy-covered brick of the carriage house. It was picturesque, beautiful, and far beyond her budget, but it was exactly the kind of place she loved. It wore its age well, and whoever owned it hadn't tried to hide that. Instead, they'd worked with it and created something charming and beautiful.

Quentin got out of the car and retrieved their bags from the back. He dropped them immediately and placed one hand on his ribs.

"I've got these, hotshot," she said and picked them up. It would have served him right to let him carry the bags and then collapse in a broken heap from it, but she just wasn't that person, even if she wanted to be sometimes.

"I can carry the damn bags, Lowey," he protested, his manly pride clearly affronted.

Her only response was an eye roll as she walked toward the door with them. She was out of patience with his he-man attitude, especially since he was so busted up it was a wonder he could even stand upright.

"Lowey!"

She glanced over her shoulder then. "You don't have to yell, asshole. I'm five feet away."

"Dammit, can you just let me be a man here?"

She relented a little bit, but not by much. "You are a man, Quentin. You just happen to be a man who got the hell beat out of him today. Now quit being a whiny little bitch and open the door."

Ignoring his bitching, grumbling, and general grumpiness as he turned the key in the lock, she stepped past him and deposited the bags on the floor just inside the door as Quentin hit the lights. The whole place was done in shades of cream and white, the ultimate shabby chic cottage decor. Throw pillows and the dark finish of the hardwood floors were the only colors in the room. She couldn't have pictured a more romantic getaway spot. *If only it was a romantic getaway.*

"There's only one bed. I'll take the couch," he said.

Part of her wanted to protest. He was beat all to hell and sleeping on a too-short couch wouldn't do him any favors. But there was just enough mean in her to be okay with it. It wouldn't kill him, she thought, but it would make him uncomfortable as hell, and *that* he deserved. "Just don't go wandering in the night...I'd hate to be the second person to have to kick the shit out of you today."

The look he gave her was pure challenge and one hundred percent pure Quentin. "You're welcome to try, sweetheart, but you're going to get more than you bargained for."

God, he was sexy. Even pissed at him, with her heart half broken by him, all she wanted to do was rip his clothes off and climb him like a damn tree. So she did the only smart thing she ever had in her life and retreated, closing the bedroom door firmly behind her.

Quentin listened to the echo of the slamming door and smiled. He'd pissed her off, and he found that oddly satisfying. It soothed his battered ego to know he could still get under her skin. God, he craved her. It'd probably kill him were he to try and do anything about it since there wasn't a single part of him that didn't hurt, but hell, it'd be worth it. Remembering just how hot it was between them, he gave a split second's thought to just knocking on that door and seeing what would happen. Whatever the cost, it would so be worth it.

Easing down onto the couch, he winced as the pain seared his ribs again. Digging his phone from his pocket, he did the one thing he hated more than anything. It was time to eat a little crow.

Pressing the speed dial number for his older brother, he braced himself for the lecture. He answered after the second ring. "What the fuck were you thinking? Do you have any idea how furious our sister is with you? How mad my wife is? And Loralei Crawford will likely never speak to any of us again!"

"I couldn't help it. He just rubbed me the wrong way," Quentin said, referring to their newly discovered half brother, Ciaran. The Irish bastard made him mad enough to chew glass. *That wasn't what had you torn up.*

Quentin ignored the little whisper in his mind, the reminder of what he thought he'd seen in Patricia's room. Every time he saw her, every time he stood over her bed, he still watched for some sign of life, some flicker of awareness. And every time he didn't see it, the anger came, the cold fury and the pain. God above, the pain of it still cut into him like a knife. He was a thirty-year-old man, but the thing he wanted more than anything in the world was just to talk with his mother.

For a split second, he'd thought it was happening. He'd seen her. A slight shifting of the muscles in her face, a tension, *an awareness*. As quickly as it had come, it had been gone, leaving him to wonder if it had ever really been there at all. The harsh reality— that he'd seen it because he wanted to and not because there was any real change in Patricia—had hit him like a rogue wave, swamping him with all the rage he tried so hard to keep locked down.

And then Ciaran, who had a chip on his shoulder that rivaled Quentin's own in size, had said something to set him off. He honestly couldn't even remember what it was. He'd just hit first, lashing out, desperately needing to funnel that fury into *anything*, anyone else. Because he knew if he kept it inside him for a second longer, he would implode.

"Well, he kicked your ass for it. It was worse than watching Rousey and Holmes," Clayton gloated.

Quentin grimaced. "Yeah, I'm aware. I feel every bit of it. The thing is, I might need his help, but if I ask—"

"Oh, that's fucking rich! You two beat the shit out of each other, and now you want to ask for a favor?"

"It's not for me," Quentin said. "A friend of mine is in a little bit of trouble. A lot of trouble actually."

Clayton went quiet for a second. "Who is this friend?"

He didn't want to tell him. It wasn't for the reasons Lowey would imagine. She'd accuse him of not thinking she was good enough. The truth was that admitting to anyone, even his brother, that he cared enough about Lowey to involve himself in her problems would open him up to something he didn't want to consider. If he let them know he was looking out for her, and then she cut him loose, it would be humiliating. But if it meant keeping her safe, he'd shout it from the rooftops and take the lumps.

"Harlow Tate," he said grudgingly. "Joey Barnes is out of jail. He destroyed The Kicking Mule today...shot the place to hell and back."

"And Silas denied his involvement completely, of course," Clayton surmised. "Why the *hell* do people keep voting for him?"

"Dear old Dad, of course," Quentin replied, his voice heavy with sarcasm. "Silas has been one of his cronies for the last decade. It served his purposes to keep Barnes in office, and we haven't been lucky enough to have an election since."

Clayton sighed heavily. "Look, I'll talk to him...but you're like his least favorite person in the world right now. So, don't hold your breath."

"I can't...the fucker broke my ribs."

Clayton laughed then. "It serves you right. Apparently, he's the Celtic version of Chuck Norris."

"You picked a fine fucking time to share that information. Here's a clue, next time I'm about to go toe-to-toe with someone, you might want to tell me if their hands are registered as a lethal weapon."

Clayton's laughter escalated to the point that he was barely intelligible on the phone before finally dying down again to a manageable level. "Don't put this shit on me. You did it...you and that smartass mouth. And I don't know why you've got such a problem with him anyway. He got just as screwed over by Samuel as we did."

Quentin couldn't answer that. The truth was, he'd taken one look at Ciaran, and he'd known him. Deep down, he'd recognized that same raised chin, those squared shoulders. But it was the challenging glint in his eyes, like he was ready to piss in the face of the world. It was like looking in a mirror, and that had pissed him off more than anything. The fucked-up psychology of trying to beat the hell out of someone because they reminded him of himself did not escape him.

"Barnes could have killed her today," he said, and the weight of that came crashing down on him.

"And why does that matter to you?" Clayton asked pointedly.

"It just does. *She* does," he admitted softly. "Talk to him. See if he'll help."

"And if he says no?"

Quentin pinched the bridge of his nose in a futile attempt to ease his aching head. "Then ask him again until he says yes. I need her safe, and I'm in no condition to handle Barnes right now."

Clayton whistled softly. "You're in so deep you can't even see daylight. You poor, sunk bastard."

The urge to deny it hit him strongly, more out of habit than because he didn't believe it, but he called it back. He might not tell Clayton everything, but he drew the line at lying to him. They'd all had more than enough lies to last them a lifetime.

"Let me know what he says."

Clayton agreed, and then Quentin ended the call without saying goodbye. He prepared himself for the sleepless night ahead, silently acknowledging that the beating he took wasn't the biggest source of his physical discomfort in that moment. It was the woman lying in a bed only a few yards away and the desperate way that he craved her.

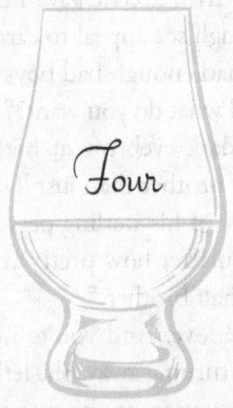

Four

It was early. Way early. So early, in fact, that it was normally the time Lowey was going to bed. Struggling out of her sleep fog, she stumbled from the bed. On her feet, she woke up just long enough to get pissed and marched to the bedroom door and then into the living room beyond. Quentin was snoring on the couch. He'd ditched his clothes and wore only a pair of black boxers that rode low enough on his hips to border on indecent. They also looked so sinfully good on him, it made her teeth ache. Even the snoring didn't dull his sexiness...god, she must be nuts.

"Get over it. Get over him and get over this, Lowey, you fucking idiot," she whispered to herself as she made her way to the door. Yanking it open, she didn't have to question that the man she was looking at was a Darcy. She didn't know him, but he and the man currently making her crazy clearly shared DNA. The same dark hair, same eyes, and chiseled bone structure were similar enough, but the fact they had matching, gigantic chips on their respective shoulders was glaringly apparent.

"Harlow Tate?"

The lilt of an Irish accent gave her pause. Yeah. He definitely had enough sex appeal to carry off that bad boy attitude. But she had enough bad boys in her life already. "Who are you, and what do you want?"

He cocked a dark eyebrow at her. "I see you share more with my half brother than just living quarters...careful, love. Any more of his sterling personality rubs off on you, and it won't matter how pretty you are. I'm Ciaran Darcy, lover boy's half brother."

"Don't call me love. And you're not exactly a peach yourself," she said, turning away. She left the door open. It was close to an invitation as she was going to give him. Darcy men in general, and the two currently in her line of sight in particular, were enough to make her lose her mind.

Ciaran whistled low. "My sympathies are leaning toward the man who shot up your bar...though, I find it hard to forgive a waste of whiskey like that."

"Jesus, you're loud!" Quentin groused from the couch as he struggled to sit up.

Lowey watched them, seeing Ciaran's satisfied smile when he took in Quentin's battered face. "You're a bit worse for wear this morning, brother."

Quentin glared at him beneath lowered brows. "I understand your natural inclination to be a dick, but do you think you can restrict it to p.m. hours?"

Ciaran settled onto the arm of an overstuffed chair. "So, your ex-con of an ex-husband is pissed because you're hooking up with this jackass?" He directed the question to Lowey, but his gaze was locked firmly on Quentin.

"No. My ex-con of an ex-husband is pissed because I sent him to prison...I wasn't inclined to take the beatings anymore or tolerate his cooking up meth in our bathroom," she explained. "He couldn't care less about Quentin or anyone else."

Ciaran shook his head. "As much as I hate to say it, your taste in men has actually improved...a bit."

Lowey's gaze was drawn to Quentin as he rose and walked toward the kitchen. He began digging through the cabinets until he emerged victorious with a can of coffee. Muscles rippled with every movement, and all she could think about was what it felt like to have him on her, in her. It made her mouth go dry and other parts of her, well, they definitely weren't dry. She looked away and found Ciaran smirking at her knowingly. It was official. As hot as the Darcy men were, she hated every last one of them.

Quentin stared impatiently at the coffee maker as water began to trickle through it. When the first bit of dark, bitter liquid splashed into the pot, he relaxed and turned to face them. "I need this if I'm going to tolerate his ass this early in the morning," he said to Lowey as he jerked his thumb in Ciaran's direction.

Taking in Ciaran's smirk, Lowey rolled her eyes again. "Can we just address why the hell he's here when we should all still be sleeping?"

Quentin looked at Ciaran then and admitted, "I had Clayton call you because if Barnes shows up, I'm in no condition to face him...and since you're the reason why, I figure you could at least pitch in."

Ciaran crossed his arms over his chest. "I'd tell you to ask nicely, but you're incapable."

"So you're here at the ass crack of dawn to turn me down?" Quentin asked as he pulled the pot from the coffee maker and poured the little bit that had brewed into a cup as it continued to drip and sizzle on the burner.

Lowey rolled her eyes. "I'm going back to bed. You all can measure your dicks without my assistance, and clearly,

I don't get to have a say in whatever is happening here anyway."

Quentin watched her walk away, noting the sway of her hips, the slight jiggle of her generously curved ass. God, was there anything sexier? She looked good coming and going.

"She catches you watching her ass that way, and she'll make the beating I gave you look like a love tap."

Quentin turned back to his half brother. He was surprised the guy had shown, honestly. If the tables had been turned, he wasn't sure he would have, and that made him uncomfortable. "So you're in?"

"I'll help," Ciaran said. "I'll pay a little visit to your darling's ex and see if I can't be a bit persuasive."

"He's probably laying low after yesterday," Quentin offered. It was the most civil comment he'd offered from the beginning.

Ciaran grinned. "I find people, Quentin. That's what I do. You might want to get those ribs looked at. Those bruises have turned nasty."

Quentin watched him walking out and muttered under his breath, "Dickhead."

Gulping the coffee and ignoring the burn, he crossed to the bedroom door and knocked. "We have to go into Lexington."

She opened the door, and while she was technically covered, he knew her body well enough to know exactly what was hidden beneath that slinky robe.

"You have to go to Lexington," she said.

"Until Barnes is back in jail or fearful enough of it to behave, you go where I go," he said.

"You're not exactly in any condition to protect me, Quentin. You can barely stand up," she snapped.

"Then you're going with me so that I won't have to drive myself in my present compromised state," he replied evenly. He wasn't leaving her there alone, and he had a meeting that couldn't be rescheduled.

Caught by her own argument, she just glared at him. Finally, after the tension in the silence built to an uncomfortable level, she relented. "I can be ready in half an hour."

"Don't use all the hot water," he said.

She glanced down at him, her eyes traveling over his body until she reached the unmistakable evidence of exactly how she affected him. "It looks like you could use a cold shower anyway!"

Quentin shook his head, even as he stepped closer to her and whispered in her ear, "I could dip my whole body in ice water. and it wouldn't make a damn bit of difference...but you keep looking at me like that, Lowey, and you're not gonna be in that shower alone."

The door slammed in his face as she retreated, the sound of it echoing through the room. Quentin dropped his chin to his chest and mentally went down the list of why it would be a disaster to go after her. Pushing Lowey was a necessity. Pushing her too far would destroy any chance of finally getting it right. It was that thought that prompted him to walk away and to sink down onto the couch and ignore just how much he wanted her.

Five

Ciaran knocked on the door of the Darcy house. He held a bouquet and a box of chocolates and tried for an expression of contrition. He wasn't sorry that he'd beat the shit out of Quentin. He'd deserved it. But he was sorry that by losing his temper, by letting the asshole get under his skin, he'd ruined the holiday for Mia. He truly did want to build a relationship with his siblings, and he'd put that on the line because he couldn't control his temper.

It was Bennett who answered the door. He looked at the flowers and the box of candy and grinned. "You're not getting off that easy."

"It's an expression of goodwill," Ciaran replied. "I fully intend to grovel along with it."

Bennet shook his head and stepped back. "She's pissed, man. Like *really* pissed. I thought I was the only one who could make her that mad...but you and Quentin —dude."

Given that she was already ticked, Ciaran decided to come clean. "I am here to apologize, but I'm also here to get some information from the two of you. I'd have asked Quentin, but frankly he's in no condition to talk. I might have overdone it a bit yesterday."

"Just a bit? Really?"

That voice coming from deep within the house was Mia's, and she sounded not just angry, but cold. If there was one thing Ciaran had learned in his life, when women sounded like that, he'd be paying for a while.

Bennett stepped aside and let him in. Mia was in the study just off the foyer, the room having long been converted into a room for her mother, Patricia. It made Ciaran instantly uncomfortable to walk into that room. Death he could deal with, but what had happened to Patricia Darcy was his definition of hell. Being confronted with the sad and horrible condition of a woman he'd secretly hated, secretly blamed for years, was a grim reminder that there were things far worse than death.

As a child, he'd built a hundred fantasies to explain why his father was not there, was not a part of his life. For years, he'd laid the blame squarely on the shoulders of the broken woman now lying in that bed. Guilt wasn't something he was accustomed to. He'd done a lot of horrible things in his life, but recalling the times he'd wished her dead so his father would be free, even if those wishes had been made in ignorance, they dug at him.

He placed the flowers and the chocolates on the table near Mia and settled onto one of the chairs scattered about the room. "I am sorry. I let my temper get the better of me...but if it helps at all, I'm here asking questions because I'm trying to help Quentin with a problem he has."

"What?" Mia asked sarcastically, her eyebrows raised and her tone impossibly sharp. "You're driving him to the emergency room?"

Ciaran dropped his head to his chest. It was that gesture, one so eerily similar to just what Quentin and Clayton did when they were feeling contrite, that prompted her to relent.

"How are you helping him?" she asked.

"It's about a friend of his...Harlow Tate. Apparently, her ex-husband is a bit of a jackass. The thing I need to know is where to find this particular jackass," he said.

She cocked her head to the side, considering the implications of what he'd said. She'd known that Quentin was seeing someone, even if he had been particularly closed-mouthed about who it was. But Harlow Tate was the last person she'd expected. "So, go back a little...Quentin and Lowey? Are you sure about this?"

Ciaran knew then that he was in, a little bit of gossip could sweeten any deal. "They were staying at Ash Grove. In the carriage house. He was sleeping on the couch, I assume because he's been a dick. But she's pissed at him. And if a man can piss a woman off, there's clearly a relationship there."

"Huh," she said, considering it for a moment. She could see it, oddly enough. They couldn't have been more different on the surface, except for the giant chips on their shoulders. But maybe that's what Quentin needed—a woman who wouldn't bow and scrape and be bowled over by his charm and good looks. Lowey Tate was drop-dead gorgeous and took no crap from anyone. If they continually butted heads with one another, then maybe they could stop butting heads with the rest of the world.

"Why are you doing this, *really*?" she asked.

"Because Quentin wasn't the only dickhead yesterday," he replied. "I'm sorry I ruined your Thanksgiving. And I'm sorry that whatever visions you had of us having a happy family reunion were ruined by us behaving like savages...now tell me where I can find this Joseph Barnes so that I can go behave like a savage in someone else's front yard."

Mia laughed in spite of herself. Her new brother was too charming for his own good or hers. And he and Quentin were like two peas in a pod. It was no wonder they had clashed. "First off, it's Joey. No one would ever call him anything as dignified as Joseph. He's a moron. A violent moron, but a moron, nonetheless. He's probably at his mama's house out on Hwy 12. But I'd be careful. The only thing lengthier than his rap sheet is his family tree. He's got a lot of cousins, and they all nest together like rats."

"Duly noted. Thank you for the warning," he said and rose from the chair. "If we do this at Christmas, I promise to behave."

"And Quentin? What if he doesn't?"

Ciaran shrugged. "That's not really up to me. I can only promise you that I won't take a swing at him...even if he begs for it."

"Give me the keys," Lowey said.

Quentin looked at her in horror as he pulled the keys in close to his chest. "I'm fine to drive."

She laughed and shook her head. "You said you needed me to drive you...so, I'm going to drive you. And *yes*, Quentin, that means you have to trust me with your baby."

No one drove his car. *Ever*. But he'd used that as an excuse to keep her with him for the day, and there was no graceful way to get out of it. So, with great reluctance, he pressed the keys into her hand. If he let his linger just a second longer than necessary, if his fingertips brushed against the tender crease in her palm, and if even that simple touch set him on fire, it was all worth it to see the slight shiver that arced through her.

Lowey brushed past him and climbed behind the wheel. Quentin winced as she adjusted the seat. It would take forever to get that right again. He knew he had issues. When it came to being set in his ways, well, Quentin accepted that particular ship had sailed long ago. Patricia had laughed at him for it as a boy, teasing him about it. And yet when she'd served his dinner, none of the food on his plate had touched. She'd tolerated his eccentricities with good humor and patience. Recalling that moment the day before when he'd thought she'd been aware of his presence, he felt the words bubbling up inside him.

"I thought—" He stopped abruptly. Telling Lowey about Patricia, about what he'd thought he saw the day before would be a mistake. He didn't talk about Patricia to anyone, not even to his siblings.

"You thought what?" she asked, adjusting the mirrors.

Every fucking thing in his car was going to be perfect for her, and he'd be struggling for months to get it put back the way he liked it. And she was enjoying it. He could see it in the gleam in her eyes.

"When I was in my mother's room yesterday...I thought she looked at me," he admitted grudgingly. Just saying it out loud made him feel like an idiot. It had been more than ten years. "It's stupid," he added. "If she was ever going to wake up, it would have happened before now."

The teasing glint in her eyes disappeared. "I'm sorry, Quentin...I can't even imagine what that feels like. My own mother was a lost cause. The best thing she ever did for me was drop me on my grandparents' doorstep before she ran off. But I remember your mom. When I was little, I remember her. Seeing her in town, always dressed to the nines but never snooty or mean the way some of those women were."

He smiled. "She loved clothes. And shopping...God above, she could shop for days."

"She was good to me," Lowey said sadly. "A lot of people in town looked down on my Papaw because of what he did...the bar. All of it. But I remember this time when I was running down Main Street, right on the sidewalk like a wild thing, and I fell. I tore half the skin off my knee. And a bunch of those women just stood there and shook their head like 'is it any wonder with how she is being raised.'"

He grinned. "And you got one of Mama's famous pep talks, didn't you?"

"I did," she agreed. "She walked over to me, picked me up, and brushed the tears off my cheeks. That's when she told me to be tough, even when it hurt, especially in front of people who would enjoy seeing me cry. And then she took me to Partin's for an ice cream and drove me home to my Papaw. Everyone in that bar was gawking when she marched me inside."

Quentin couldn't help but laugh. He could picture every bit of it. And even though it tickled him in so many ways to think of his mother, the lady to end all ladies, walking into a dive bar called The Kicking Mule, it still hurt. It chipped away at the hard shell he'd built around all the pain inside him.

"I bet she was mad as fire and gave your granddad the what-for," he said.

Lowey shook her head and smiled sadly. "She didn't actually. It was about a year after we'd lost Mamaw, and she just told him how sorry she was, and how it had to be so hard for him having a little girl there that he didn't know what to do with...then they had a drink together, and the next thing I knew I was taking cotillion lessons that I know, now at least, we couldn't possibly have afforded."

It was so typical of his mother that it cut him to the quick. "I miss her. I miss her every goddamn day of my life...and I get so fucking mad. I'm a horrible person, Lowey."

"You're not a horrible person, Quentin! Not for being mad because of what happened to her!"

"I am a horrible person, Lowey," he said softly, "Because I'm mad *at* her. Because I think, all the fucking time, that we'd all be better off if she'd just died. Then there would have been an end to it. There'd have been a point we could have just moved on from. But we're all still stuck in limbo right along with her."

He'd never admitted that to anyone. Those words, those thoughts, had eaten away at him for years, and he was afraid to look over at her, afraid to see the way she'd look at him after.

When she finally spoke, her voice was soft, and for Lowey, it was impossibly tender. "That doesn't make you horrible. The truth of the matter is, Quentin, what happened to your mother is worse than death. And what you've had to deal with—it's worse than grieving for someone who died. Because the world lets you fall apart then. People stand back and let you just wail and scream and carry on. But for this, they tell you to be strong, to be there for your family, to pray because God never gives you more than you can handle. Well, I call bullshit on that. What you've had, with Samuel and with your mama, that's more than anybody should ever have to handle."

Six

The drive into Lexington was quiet. After his earlier admission, he'd retreated into himself. Lowey understood that. She was still amazed that he'd opened up to her at all. Quentin didn't ever talk about *feelings*. Hell, he didn't acknowledge having them. Just moods. And God above, he could be a moody bastard. But at least now she understood why. There was so much pain trapped inside him, a lot of guilt and misery he just didn't know how to let go of even to save himself. And she was nobody's savior. The last time she'd thought she could save a man he'd nearly killed her.

"Where are we headed exactly?" she asked as they approached New Circle Road.

"Downtown. I'm meeting someone at the Hyatt."

She rolled her eyes. "Business or pleasure? Do I need to run you by an ATM first, so you'll have cash to pay for whatever services are being rendered?"

"What the hell are you talking about? I'm not meeting a hooker!"

"Then stop being so damn vague. Not everything has to be a mystery, Quentin!"

He sighed and leaned his head back against the seat. "Fine. I'm meeting an old friend of mine who may be interested in investing in Fire Creek. Now that we have Samuel's share of the company in our control, we're looking to make some changes and trying to expand."

"That was very informative," she replied. "Thank you...you know, I have to ask, is it me that you keep things from specifically, or are you just this closed off with everyone?"

"I just told you something that I've never told anyone else in my life. And you are accompanying me to a meeting that could literally change the course of not just my family's business but our entire town. What do you think?"

Lowey turned off New Circle onto Nicholasville Road and headed toward Main Street. When he put it in those terms, it felt big. Momentous even. And that made her equal parts uncomfortable and hopeful. In all, it was just an awkward as hell position to be in.

"I think I don't know what prompted your sudden openness, and it terrifies me," she admitted. "I can't afford for you to suddenly be the man I need...because we both know it won't last. You'll go back to being a closed-mouthed, hard-hearted son of a bitch, and I'll be stuck pining for you all over again."

"Did you pine for me?"

Shit. She should never have said that. It was bad enough she'd done it. Admitting to it just added humiliation on top of it. Brushing it off as if it wasn't important, she replied, "For an hour or two. Then I got over it."

"I didn't." He said it softly, his voice pitched low. But in the quiet confines of the car, it still resounded like a shot. It was what she'd wanted him to say, what she'd wanted so desperately to hear. Trusting him wasn't easy though. Trusting anyone wasn't easy for her, and he'd already burned her once.

"Don't do this, Quentin. Not now," she implored. "Neither one of us is in a place for this."

He continued, never taking his eyes off her and speaking so resolutely that it just cut straight through her. "It wasn't just an hour or two. I have missed you every goddamn day. I regretted walking out that door the second it closed behind me."

"Then you should have thought about that before you walked out!" she said, turning the car into one of the parking structures near the hotel. "I'll wait for you here."

He reached for the door handle but paused. "This is not over. You and me...we're not over."

"You're starting to sound a hell of a lot like Joey Barnes," she said. "You don't get to decide for me!"

He looked back at her then, his gaze direct and challenging. "Then tell me that you don't feel it...you tell me that, and I'll walk away whether I want to or not."

She couldn't make herself utter the words even though she wanted to. The need to say them was so strong that they burned on her lips, but she couldn't force them out. After a moment of torturous silence, he gave a slight nod that was packed full of "I told you so" and got out of the car.

"Asshole," she muttered. Even then, her gaze was locked firmly on his perfectly sculpted ass as he walked away from her.

Quentin walked into the hotel and headed directly for the restaurant where Deacon Mallory was waiting for him. They'd gone to college together. Partied and drank together. Somehow, they'd mostly sobered up and got their shit together in tandem as well. Or as together as his could be, Quentin thought, since emotionally, he was about as fucked up as any one person could be.

As he approached the table, Deacon let out a low whistle. "I hope she was worth it," he said with a grin.

They were friends, and Quentin could tell him that it wasn't over a woman. But then he'd have to tell him that it was about family drama instead, and since he was there to get him to invest in the *family* business, it seemed like a stupid move to him. So, he just smiled and kept his mouth shut as he eased into the chair. His ribs hurt. Everything hurt, but it wasn't as bad as the day before. He felt like his lungs could actually expand.

"A gentleman never tells," he replied smoothly.

Deacon nodded. "Find me a gentleman and we'll ask just to be sure...have you got the numbers for me?"

Quentin pulled out his phone and flipped through the numerous documents on it until he found the proposal. "It's all there. Profits were down, but you know why. We talked about that. I've also included the plans for expanded production and distribution, but that's a long-haul return. This will make you money, but it's going to take at least five years before you see any of it."

"I know what I'm getting into here, Quentin. I know about your fucked-up father and what he's done...I also know that you wouldn't try to sell me on this unless you were convinced that it would work. I've always loved Kentucky...loved it since I played college ball here. But I know that if I want to fit here, to make a home here, I have to be part of something and not just an observer.

Buying into Fire Creek gives me that. So, I'm in. Send the contracts to my attorney, and we'll get the financing sorted out...by the way, I'm buying a house in Fontaine. Have an appointment to look at it this afternoon."

Quentin shook his head. "No half measures with you...ever. Are you sure you want to live in Fontaine? Your entertainment options are pretty limited."

"As long as I can get beer and SportsCenter, I'm good to go."

Quentin rose to his feet, as did Deacon Mallory. They shook hands. "I didn't realize your standards had lowered so much."

"I'm too old to party without jeopardizing my good looks," Deacon answered with a grin.

"Cocky bastard." Quentin shoved his phone back into his pocket and turned to walk away.

Deacon called out. "I know you weren't fighting over a woman...'cause you don't do that. But I also know you well enough to know that one's got you tied up in knots."

Quentin shrugged, though it cost him. God above, he *hurt*. "Just wait until you meet the one who does that to you."

Deacon grinned. "I can't fucking wait."

Seven

Ciaran eased his truck to a stop at the end of the formerly gravel, but now mostly mud, driveway of the Barnes's house. House was probably pushing it. The ramshackle trailers, all cobbled together, looked more like something out of a Mad Max movie than like something that would be sitting in the middle of bourbon country.

Picking up the file from the seat beside him, he skimmed the documents and photos inside. Yes, he was helping out Quentin to appease Mia, but he was also helping out his soon-to-be brother-in-law, Matt Crawford. It seemed that during his recent stint at Blackburn, Joey had shared a cell with a talkative Russian fellow by the name of Sergei. And since Sergei was no longer talking to anyone, Joey Barnes might be their best shot for getting more intel on the original source of the drugs Sergei and his associates had been peddling.

Getting out of the truck, he walked casually up the driveway, as if he had every right to be there. Sneaking up on paranoid-ass drug dealers was worse than doing a night drop in a war zone. A large dog chained in the yard growled and barked as he made his way onto the porch. Boards shifted beneath his weight, and he wondered how the whole thing didn't just fall through.

Ciaran knocked on the door and waited. Then he knocked again. From inside, he could hear the shuffling of trash, bottles being knocked over. They might have had a party, or they might just live that way. He didn't know, and he honestly didn't care.

Through the closed door he heard someone shout. "Answer the fucking door, bitch!"

Ciaran clenched his fists at his side. He'd never spoken to a woman that way in his life, and it pissed him off to hear it from someone else.

When the door did finally open, it wasn't some strung-out young girl like he'd expected. The woman was probably middle-aged, and yet she could have been a hundred. Rail thin, her gray hair tied back in a messy knot and dressed in clothes so old and threadbare it was a wonder they didn't simply disintegrate on the spot—she was probably the saddest creature he'd ever laid eyes on.

"Can I help you?" she asked.

Her voice was rough from chain-smoking for years, but still timid and weak. She ducked her head and wouldn't make eye contact with him, but it allowed the bruise on her cheekbone to stand out in stark relief.

"I'm looking for Joey...I need to talk to him," Ciaran replied evenly, the whole time wondering if Joey was responsible for that bruise.

"He's not here," she replied and started to close the door.

Ciaran caught it with his palm, keeping her from closing it in his face. "Where can I find him?"

"I don't know. He's a grown man and doesn't have to tell me where he goes or when he'll be home."

"But he will be home?" Ciaran demanded.

She sighed again, heavy and broken. "Maybe. I don't know. He's been running wild ever since he got out...it was better when he was still locked up. Least then I knew where he was."

"Don't say another damn word!"

The man, if he could be called that, who'd been yelling and cursing inside was making his way to the door. It wasn't her husband, Ciaran realized. It was another of her worthless sons. The wifebeater, which was ironic, the dirty jeans, gauged ears, neck tattoos, and sideways hat were pretty indicative that he didn't have any sort of legitimate employment. But the brand-new truck parked in the yard clearly said he had money.

"What the fuck do you want with my brother?" he demanded.

"I want to ask him why he shot up Harlow Tate's bar," Ciaran said. "And then I want to ask him, politely, to not do it again."

The little punk laughed. "That's between him and his old lady...ain't nothing to you."

Ciaran smiled. "Since they are divorced, you can't really call her his old lady. And it's very much something to me as she's now dating my brother."

"I don't give two shits who she's dating...she belongs to Joey."

"Kyle, don't cause trouble!" the mother warned.

"He's the one causin' trouble," Kyle replied. "Walking up to my door and telling me what me and mine can and can't do. That shit don't play."

Ciaran, already disgusted by the way the little shit had talked to his mother, reached out and grabbed him by the throat. His fingers pressed the carotid artery on one side and his thumb on the other, with just enough force to leave him weak and disoriented. If he pressed harder, he could knock him out cold in under ten seconds, or he could kill him. "I asked you a very polite question. You can give me a very polite answer, or I can snap your neck like a goddamn twig."

Ciaran kept his eyes on the mother. It didn't matter that her son was an asshole, he was still her son. Beaten down, abused, she would still defend him with her dying breath.

"Now, Mrs. Barnes, tell me where to find Joey. I only want to talk to him."

"Don't hurt him," she said. "They're good boys! They just got their daddy's temper is all!"

"I will do my best to avoid it," he replied. They both knew that wouldn't be possible, but he made the offer regardless.

"He's in Lexington...staying with his cousin down off Fourth Street."

"The cousin's name?"

"Tommy. Tommy Barnes," she replied.

Ciaran released Kyle who stumbled backward and sank to the ground looking dazed. "You should leave them. Every one of them. They don't appreciate you, and they're only going to treat you worse the longer you stay."

She folded her arms over her chest. "They're my kids. And they don't hit me."

"Just your husband, then?"

She didn't say anything more. Ciaran shook his head as he walked away. You couldn't save someone who didn't want to be saved, he reminded himself. They had bigger problems to deal with at any rate. Tracking down Joey Barnes, finding out what information he had on the

Russians, and making it perfectly clear that even if the law didn't stop him from targeting Lowey Tate, someone would.

The drive back to Ash Grove Farm was quiet. Lowey wasn't saying much, and Quentin felt like he'd talked more in the last two days than he had in his whole damn life. At the very least, he'd said more meaningful things than he had in his whole damn life. Evasion. Misdirection. Distraction. Those were the tactics he normally preferred. Laying it all out on the line was much more Clayton's style than it was his. But the last year had changed things for them both. Clayton had decided to become more like Samuel in order to bring him down.

As for himself, he'd looked in the mirror one day and saw a hell of a lot more of Samuel Darcy staring back at him than he'd ever wanted to. He was using people, getting what he wanted from them and then walking away. And that wasn't the kind of man he wanted to be. It sure as hell wasn't the kind of man Patricia had been raising him to be.

One could argue that at twenty years old, he was already raised by the time she'd had her accident. But the truth was that no twenty-year-old had achieved actual manhood yet. He'd been a boy in a man's body, and at thirty, he'd recognized that he wasn't much better. Drinking too much, partying too much, and going through women like they were disposable. That included the one beside him, or at least he'd wanted it to.

There was something about Lowey, though, something that had just crawled inside him and wouldn't let go. For the past two months, he'd driven by her bar at least daily. Every time he'd been tempted to stop, tempted to grovel, and pride wouldn't let him. It had taken getting his shit handed to him by a brother he'd just met to humble him enough to go in there and face her, to face what he'd done.

The night that everything had gone south played over in his mind. It had started like any other. He'd worked late, and after finally leaving the office, he'd headed to The Kicking Mule for a drink. When the crowd had thinned out and Lowey could leave everything to the bartenders, she'd slipped away to her little apartment upstairs, and he'd followed.

It had hit him then, walking up those stairs behind her, that she'd become a habit. Coming to her house every night, sinking into the welcoming heat of her, it was more than just scratching an itch. Everything he did in the course of his day was just killing time until he could get back there and be with her again.

That's when the panic had set in.

He'd done the only thing then that he could. He'd lashed out.

"This isn't working for me anymore," he'd said.

She'd stopped at the top of the stairs and looked back at him. "What the hell does that mean?"

"Look, Lowey, we both knew when this started this wasn't a permanent thing for us. We're just not long-term kind of people." The doucheyness of his behavior was haunting him as he remembered the look in her eyes. All the life, all the fire, had just faded from them. And having her look at him with such cool loathing had made him want to squirm even then.

"With all due respect, Quentin Darcy, you've been way more interested in my ass than my mind. Why don't

47

you ask a few questions before you decide you know just who I am and just what it is that I want? The answers might surprise you!"

"I don't want to hurt you," he'd said. But he did. He wanted to hurt her badly enough that she'd never want him again. That bridge had to be burned because he'd never have the strength just to walk away from her on his own.

She'd turned then and walked back down the stairs, pausing on the one right above him so that they were eye to eye. "You might not want to, but you will...because you might not be a long-term kind of person, but I am. And the fact that you'd assume I'm not, tells me all I need to know."

"What the hell does that mean?"

She'd looked so sad then, but also completely resolute. "It means that I know my place in this town. I know how people look down on me. I just let myself forget for a moment that you were one of them...so go on and go. I'll be damned to hell and back before I try to stop you."

Standing there, watching her walk away from him, knowing that when she reached the top of those stairs, the door would close and lock between them, he'd let it happen. He'd been the one thing he despised above all else, the one thing he'd lied to himself about for most of his life. He'd been a coward.

Pulling himself back to the present and to the woman who sat beside him driving the car that he prized above almost anything else in the world, he said, "We should grab some food while we're out. There's nothing at the farm, and I don't want to cook."

She snorted. "You don't cook."

"I do if it's prepackaged and frozen. I know how to turn on the oven, Harlow."

"I'll cook," she said. "We'll hit the Fresh Market before we get out of town. But you're buying."

It wasn't exactly an olive branch, but at least it wasn't cold and uncomfortable silence. Eventually, they'd have to talk about it. Eventually he'd have to tell her that he ran like a scolded dog because she'd gotten so deep inside him that it terrified him. It wasn't a conversation he looked forward to, but more than that, he was terrified it wouldn't make a damn bit of difference. So, he turned his attention to another question that was bugging the shit out of him.

"We've never talked about your ex...what is this really all about, Lowey?"

She clammed up then. He could see it in the firm set of her jaw. She would acknowledge that he almost killed her following their divorce, but she never talked about the marriage itself, she never shared details. And he had to know.

"Why did Joey Barnes come back and shoot up your bar?"

"Because he's an asshole," she replied stiffly.

"He's an asshole on parole, and he knows that Silas can only do so much to protect him. Why take that risk, Lowey? What was in it for him?"

"Why will you not leave this alone?" she asked. "Does it really matter why?"

"Yes, it does. And if he's doing this after the divorce, what the hell was the marriage like?"

Eight

Joey Barnes wasn't a topic she cared to discuss *ever*. No one knew the full extent of what he'd put her through, of what she'd allowed him to do to her, because she was too embarrassed and too ashamed to ask for help. To admit those things to Quentin was more than she could bear, but she also knew it was necessary.

"Tell me, Lowey. Or I'll find out on my own."

"You know the day the divorce decree was final, he basically lost it. He came to the bar at closing time, waited until everyone had left and then came in and—" She stopped, unable to say all the things he'd done to her. The torment of kneeling in front of him while he held a gun to her head, while he debated with her all the reasons he ought to kill her, or the reasons he should just, as he'd put it, fuck up her pretty face until no one would ever want her again.

"I know enough about that," he said. "But that wasn't the only time, was it?"

"No," she admitted, speaking slowly as she uncovered some of her most painful memories. "He started beating the hell out of me almost as soon as I married him...I was eighteen. Didn't know any better. Married him and let him move me into the shithole his family lives in. The black eyes, the twisted arms, the bruised ribs, the split lips...I stayed inside most of the time because it was easier just not to see people than to try and camouflage it or have to lie. I didn't want my Papaw to know how bad it was."

It was difficult to put into words, but she knew she had to try. "With him, it wasn't that he was jealous. It was that he *owned* me—body and soul. If he wanted to hit me, he did. If he wanted to lock me up and starve me, he did. If he wanted sex, and I didn't feel inclined...well, that wasn't really an option."

She watched him for a response, noting the tension in his jaw, his clenched fists. He didn't say anything, but she understood that. There was no appropriate response to what she'd just said to him.

"How did you get out?"

Lowey shrugged. "He thought he owned me, and it never occurred to him that I would turn him in for doing something illegal...I called Matt Shepherd, and he put me in touch with someone from the DEA, and they busted him while he was out of the house. He got three years, and I got out. While he was in prison, I filed for divorce and moved back in with my grandfather."

It sounded so simple when she said it. None of that took into account the terror, the fear, she'd lived with every moment of every day, waiting for him to get out, waiting for him to come for her. Then her grandfather had died, and she'd been alone. Completely and totally alone. And she couldn't tell him that the very reason he'd appealed to her was because he would never want to own or possess her. The commitment phobia that had broken her heart had been one of his most appealing qualities.

"So he got out, and then he came for you," he replied.

"Yeah. Within a week of his release, he was at the bar... but I'm not telling you about that night. I've relived it enough already, and I'm not going back to do it again." Maybe it was cowardly, but she was okay with that. If she told him the whole truth, he'd look at her differently. And she didn't want his pity. Never that.

Changing the tone of the conversation, she said, "It seriously pisses me off that he got more time for cooking meth than he did for trying to murder me."

"It more than pisses me off," he said. "I promise you, Lowey, one way or another, he's not getting near you again."

"Don't make promises, Quentin. We both know that's not your thing."

"I don't make many promises, Lowey, but when I make them, I keep them. He's never getting near you again. Count on it."

She sighed then. "He's been in contact—even from jail. Usually through his brothers and his cousins. For the past year, ever since he went back to jail. They blame me... all of them blame me."

"It stops today."

There was no point in telling him that she had her doubts. She'd accepted last year that when she died, it would be at Joey Barnes's hands. But that didn't mean she'd go down without a fight. Never again.

Joseph Allen Barnes sipped his beer and watched the rather long-in-the-tooth stripper sashay across the small stage and wrap her body around the pole. She might have been old, but she could sure as hell move, he thought with a grin.

Reaching into his pocket for a few singles, he waved them toward the stripper. He wondered what he could get her to do for the hundred-dollar bill he had tucked into his wallet.

After he'd tucked the bills into her G-string, she offered him a wave and a smile before sauntering back to the pole. His appreciation of the view she offered was interrupted by someone smacking the back of his head, hard.

"What the fuck did you do?"

Joey looked back to see his cousin standing behind him. Tommy looked pissed.

"What the hell did you do that for? I ain't done nothing."

Tommy sat down and took the beer Joey had been working on, draining the bottle. "Your mama called and says some dude came to the trailer looking for you. Claims to be a Darcy and says Lowey's hooked up with another one of 'em."

Joey's fists clenched at his sides. *Fucking whore.* "She's my ex. None of my damn business who she hooks up with, now is it?"

Tommy laughed. "Try that with somebody else, ass wipe. I know what you did to her bar, and I know you used my damn gun to do it. I found the empty box of shells!"

Joey shrugged it off. Silas was taking care of it. "They can't prove it."

"It's the goddamn Darcys. They don't *have* to prove it! Do I need to remind you about the kind of people you got us tangled up with? These Russians are bad dudes, Joey. Taking over distribution for them was your idea...

you and your damn *dead* cell mate. I shoulda known better than to listen to a fuck-up like you!"

Joey shoved him then, sending the chair tipping backward and Tommy sprawling on the floor. "Are you making money? Yeah, well then shut up! I hooked you into this deal...but I owe that bitch, and she fucking well owes me! She's gonna pay. Whatever it takes!"

Tommy had just made it to his feet when the bouncers wandered over, looming nearby. They weren't too interested in guys beating the hell out of each other. That was less of a problem than when patrons went after the girls. Dusting himself off, Tommy shook his head. "You're gonna get us both killed. We've got bigger shit to worry about than who your ex-wife is fucking!"

"She sent me to prison!" Joey shouted. "You think I care whose dick she's ridin'?"

Tommy shook his head. "Stay focused, Joey. Stay focused, or we're both gonna wind up with a bullet in our heads!"

"I'm not fucking this up, Tommy! We're gonna get the drugs, we're gonna get 'em to the distributors, and when it's done, that bitch will pay."

Tommy sat back and scrubbed his hands over his face. "This ain't gonna end well."

Nine

Back at the carriage house, Quentin held the door for Lowey. They hadn't said much of anything after her confession. He was still trying to process it himself. The harsh realities she'd laid out for him were beyond what he'd imagined. Yes, he'd known Joey Barnes was an abusive dick. But knowing her, how strong she was and how little shit she took from anyone, he'd just never stopped to consider that it might have been more than an isolated incident.

"Stop it," she hissed.

"Stop what?"

"Stop looking at me like I'm some fragile little thing on the verge of breaking! I'm not. He did what he did, and I got through it. I *lived*. End of story, Quentin."

He could hear the frustration in her voice. But what the hell was he supposed to do? She'd just admitted to him that she'd been put through every kind of torment imaginable by the sadistic fuck, and that wasn't supposed to have an effect on him? Maybe he wasn't good at the whole commitment thing, and maybe he would never be a good bet for the long haul, but that didn't change his feelings for her. It sure as hell didn't change the fact that he wanted to find Joey Barnes and rip the fucker's spine out. "Doesn't seem like the end to me," he said. "Clearly it doesn't seem like the end to him either, or he wouldn't be plotting his revenge!"

"I'm not a damsel in distress, and you're sure as hell nobody's white knight!"

"Damn it, Lowey, why can't you accept the fact that I'm here for you?"

"For now," she shot back. "And I don't need temporary, Quentin. I'll get a taxi to take me back to Fontaine. I'm not staying here with you anymore!" She turned away and stormed through the small guest house, heading for the bedroom where she'd left her things.

"It doesn't change the way I see you," he said. It was an instinct more than anything that prompted him to say it, to recognize that she felt weakened, vulnerable, because of the things she'd admitted to him in the car. "I still think you're a badass. And I think any man, woman, or hell-spawned demon foolish enough to tangle with you deserves whatever they get...and I still want you. Because there's nothing that you could say or do that will ever change that."

Lowey whirled on him then, snatched the porcelain dish off the table, and hurled it at his head. He ducked to the side and winced as pain stabbed his ribs. She was hurting, and he knew it, but that didn't mean he'd just let her take potshots at him. In three strides, he reached her. Gripping her arms, he pressed her back against the wall. He wasn't hurting her, but he'd be damned if he was going to let her hurt him.

"I'm not the one you're mad at," he said.

"Fuck you."

"If that's an invitation—"

She screeched at him. It was all rage and fury and the years of pain that she'd tamped down, locked away, and refused to ever deal with. He was all too familiar with it. But fighting her wouldn't help and keeping her pinned against the wall indefinitely wasn't really an option. So Quentin did the only thing he could think of. He kissed her and prayed like hell she wouldn't bite his lip off.

The kiss caught her off guard, not because it was unexpected. She'd lost count of the number of times they'd argued, then fallen on each other like rabid animals. But this was something else. The gentle press of his lips, the soft and sensual glide of his tongue, took her breath away. But the tenderness in his touch cut through her. It touched that inner part of her that she kept locked away.

Tears burned her eyes, and she could feel the lump forming in her throat as she tried to fight them back. She failed miserably. The tears spilled over, streaming down her cheeks as her hands clenched the fabric of his shirt, pushing him away and holding onto him desperately all at the same time.

When he pulled back, staring down at her with such tenderness and such longing, it cut her to the quick. "Don't do this to me," Lowey implored.

"What am I doing, baby?" Quentin asked softly as he wound the fall of her hair around his hand.

"Don't make me need you when you're never going to stay."

He didn't say anything, but he dropped his head until his forehead rested against hers. His hands slipped lower, resting on her hips. They stood like that for the longest time, like two exhausted boxers in the last round. Bloodied, bruised, and worn out, offering as much solace as punishment to one another.

"No promises...I can't tell you this is forever," Quentin said. "But I can tell you that you mean more to me than any woman ever has. You're in me, Lowey Tate... down to the blood and bone."

She had longed to hear things like that from him, to have some inkling that she was more to him than just a good time—a convenient and willing woman to scratch an itch.

"I can't do this with you," she said, aware of the note of desperation in her voice. She hoped he was too. Her sanity was dependent on him recognizing just how sincere she was. He had the power to hurt her in ways that Joey Barnes never had. Yes, he'd hit her. He'd tortured and tormented her physically, but he'd never broken her heart. Quentin Darcy could do that and far more easily than either of them had ever imagined.

"It isn't a choice, Lowey. This thing between us is inevitable."

It was all the warning she had. He moved suddenly, backing her against the wall, his hands delving into her hair. Then his lips were on hers.

Being kissed by Quentin Darcy was unlike anything she'd ever known before. Pleasure flooded her, stimulating her senses—the taste of him on her tongue, the scent of him, the hard press of his body against hers.

Then his hands were sliding over her, mapping the curves of her waist, her hips, before his palms settled heavily on the cheeks of her behind. He squeezed, kneading her flesh, and pressing against her so that she could feel just how much he wanted her.

He was temptation personified, and she was too weak to fight it. Giving in not just gracefully but eagerly, she reached for his tie, loosening it and then tackling the buttons of his shirt. When the fabric parted, she slid her hands inside, tracing the hard ridges of muscle, the crisp hair that covered his chest. She scraped her nails lightly over the flat disk of his nipple and smiled as he hissed out a breath.

"Witch," he murmured against her lips.

"I can stop if you want me to," she offered.

"God, no," he whispered hoarsely. "Do it again."

She did and got the same response. How was it possible that stoking his desire only intensified her own?

"Take me to bed," she said. "Let's just forget everything for a little while."

It took him a second to fully register what she'd said. Maybe it was the fact that none of the blood in his body was flowing to his brain, or maybe it was the fact that he hadn't expected her to relent. Whatever it was, he didn't need to be asked twice.

Carrying her to bed wasn't an option, though he wished it was. For the first time in his life, he wanted to be the man who made sweeping romantic gestures. He wanted to pick her up and carry her to bed, he wanted to surprise her with flowers, with her favorite meal, to take her out and show her off to the world, and to show her that she was worthy of that and so much more.

But bruised ribs and the very real prospect of dropping her on the floor intruded on such notions. So, instead he pulled her to him, kissed her again, and walked her backward toward the bedroom door. Luckily, the carriage house was small enough that nothing was too far away. Patience was in short supply and dwindling.

Once in the bedroom, he kicked the door closed behind them and reached for the hem of her sweater, tugging it up over her hips. She raised her arms, and he pulled it over her head, exposing the lacy bra she wore beneath. God, he loved every lush curve, every inch of soft, silken skin. If he wasn't a total coward, he'd just admit that he loved her. But neither of them were ready for that. So instead, he'd just show her all the things he was too terrified to say out loud.

With slow, deliberate movements, he freed the button of her jeans and then slid the zipper down one torturous inch at a time.

"We're going to be old before you get me naked," she said with a sly smile.

"I like to unwrap my presents slowly, Lowey...I want to savor every second of it."

"Savor it a little faster, Quentin...I need you inside me."

His cock hardened to the point of agony. And she'd done it on purpose, he knew. He'd wanted to romance her, to make love to her, but like every time he was in her presence, the overwhelming *need* for Lowey simply took over. Shoving her pants down, he spun her around so that her back was pressed to his chest. He bent his head, his lips pressing against her neck. Then he bit down, his teeth scraping the skin.

She gasped, but it wasn't pain. He knew that sound, knew the pleasure that prompted it.

"I want you on your knees," he whispered hotly against her ear.

She shivered against him, and Quentin smiled. It was

what they both wanted—what they both needed. Romance would wait. After two months, he just needed to sink into the heat of her, to feel her body closing around him. It was worse than a drug, the way he wanted her. She was like an addiction for him. For the past two months, since he'd been stupid enough to walk out, she'd been on his mind every waking second and even in his dreams.

When she climbed onto the bed, kneeling in front of him, her perfect ass displayed like he'd somehow been granted the gift of living out his favorite wet dream, Quentin knew that he was sunk, no more running, no more pretending. He wanted this—he wanted her—forever.

Ten

Lowey could feel him behind her, the weight of his presence tangible even before he touched her. But then he did, his fingers digging into her hips as he pulled her back against him. The hard press of his cock against her drew a shattered moan from deep within her. She dropped her head onto the bed, arching her hips back against him, a silent entreaty for more.

"I've dreamed about you just this way." The confession rasped out of him, his voice deeper and gruffer than usual. It shivered over her and stoked the flames.

"Then, God above, Quentin...what are you waiting for?" she asked. The need to feel him moving inside her, filling her up, and taking her the way that only he could was too intense, too all-consuming, to allow for patience.

It was like she'd flipped a switch. She heard the rasp of his zipper, so loud in the silent room. Then he was there, the blunt head nudging against her as he parted her with his fingers. He slid two inside her. It was unnecessary. Foreplay, while a wonderful thing, was wholly redundant.

She'd been wet for him since the moment she'd laid eyes on him.

It wasn't pleasure, when he entered her. That was too mild a term. It was relief—intense, overwhelming, and consuming. For just a moment, it assuaged the awful need that was like a constant and unrelenting torture. Then he moved, thrusting inside her, and the need flared to biting, scratching life again. It clawed within her as her fingers clenched the bedding. She screamed his name as the tension within her suddenly ratcheted higher, to the point she felt as if she might simply shatter with it.

Each thrust, each powerful surge of his hips as he drove into her only heightened the sensation. She was crying out insensibly, her body shivering beneath his as she climbed. The sounds that escaped her were more animal than human, but she was beyond caring.

"Please," she gasped. She didn't even know what she was asking for.

His hand moved from her hip, his fingers trailing up her spine until they tangled in her hair. He closed his fist then, tugging her hair taut and pulling her head back. It changed the angle of penetration just slightly...just enough. A broken sob racked her, left her shuddering. And then he thrust into her again—harder, deeper—and she broke. Her body trembled as the pleasure washed through her, every muscle quivering as the waves crested again and again.

Lowey was still shaking when he abruptly withdrew from her. He flipped her onto her back. His hands were rough on her, but she craved that from him. She needed to feel that desperation from him, to believe, even if it was just for this moment—that he was as consumed by it as she was.

When he came down on top of her, his weight settling

between her parted thighs, he kissed her again. His mouth was hot on hers, his tongue surprisingly gentle as he slipped it between her lips. It glided tenderly against hers —soft, sweet. It wasn't the kind of kiss you got from someone who just wanted to fuck you. It was the kind of kiss you got from someone who loved you.

But there was no time to question it, no time to ask him to explain. He was sliding into her again, easing his cock inside her and thrusting deep. He pulled back then, breaking the kiss and looking down at her. Their gazes were locked together as intimately as their bodies.

It was different, she thought. *He* was different. Whatever was between them had changed, morphed into this strange thing that neither of them fully understood or was prepared to define or deal with. Then conscious thought fled, and she was left with only the ability to feel.

Quentin gritted his teeth, trying to hold back his own release until he could watch her come for him again. The need to see that, to see her head thrown back and her lips parted on a silent cry as she shuddered beneath him, was something he couldn't ignore.

Dipping his head, he pressed a kiss to the soft skin between her breasts and followed it with a lick. He could taste the salt of her skin as she strained beneath him. The muscles of her thighs trembled, her belly quivered, and he knew that she was close. He slipped one hand between their bodies, pressed one finger against her, stroking her clit with deliberate precision. Her neck arched, her head fell back, and her lips parted on a soundless cry as she clenched around him. The rhythmic clenching of her body around him pushed him over the edge. He thrust deep once more, surging into her and gritting his teeth with the force of his release as he came inside her.

Collapsing onto the bed, resting his weight on his elbow so he didn't crush her, Quentin struggled to regain his breath. Regaining his equilibrium was a lost cause. She rocked him to his soul, and he wouldn't have it any other way.

Lowey was beyond beautiful, but it wasn't just her perfect face or her curvy body that haunted his dreams that drew him to her. It was the hint of vulnerability beneath all the barbs. He wanted to take care of her, to be the man she didn't think she deserved.

"If I didn't know better," she said, rolling onto her side and curling against him, "I'd think you missed me."

He grinned as he rolled onto his side to face her. Looking at her was a joy in and of itself, but looking at her this way, with her face still flushed, her lips still swollen from his kisses, that was something special. "You know I did. And you missed me. Don't bother trying to deny it."

She turned her head to stare up at the ceiling. "I wouldn't. For better or worse, Quentin, no one makes me feel the way you do."

Quentin's grin faded slightly as he took in her profile. There was still a sadness in her, and he had to wonder if it wouldn't be there forever. Lowey had struggled her whole life. She was still struggling. At least he had his siblings, even if they did drive him crazy sometimes. She was alone in the world, and he had to live with the fact that he'd exploited that to his advantage. He'd used that to worm his way into her life with every intention of just leaving her behind when he was done.

Coming face-to-face with his own ugliness was a hard thing to do, but it was time to own it. It was time to stop hiding behind everything that he'd pretended to be, everything he'd tried to be, and just accept what he was.

"We're going to try for better. I can't promise we'll succeed," he said softly, "But I can promise to try."

"What is this, Quentin? This isn't you."

"It is," he protested. "No more walls. No more hiding. I want you, and not just for sex...amazing as it is. I want all of it. Body and soul."

She looked at him directly then, those dark eyes of hers peering right through him. He couldn't have hidden anything from her in that moment even if he wanted to.

"If I give that to you," she replied in a low, steady tone. "You have to give it back. I'm tired of this being a one-way street."

"Whatever I have, baby, and whatever I am, it's yours."

Eleven

Ciaran walked into the small, ugly brick building that housed Fontaine's Sheriff's Office. He'd been asking questions, and he had the idea that while Silas Barnes would be perfectly willing to overlook Joey busting up Lowey's place, he had serious doubts the man would be willing to overlook the massive influx of a dangerous drug into his tiny little town.

"Silas Barnes?" he asked, stepping into the office.

The ancient, bespectacled woman behind the counter jerked her head toward the closed door to her left. Her hair, teased and shellacked into a style popular in 1967, didn't move a millimeter.

Ciaran nodded his thanks and crossed the small room. He knocked on the door as he opened it, not allowing the man to send him away. He'd spent the better part of his morning running in circles trying to track down Harlow Tate's piece of shit ex-husband, and he was done. It was time to use the resources available to him.

"We need to talk," he said.

The sheriff put down his cell phone mid text and

glared at him. "Well, now that you've let yourself into my office like it's your goddamn right, who am I to say no?"

Ciaran smiled. It really didn't matter to him whether or not Silas Barnes hated his guts. "Your cousin made some interesting friends while he was at Blackburn," Ciaran began. "The kind of friends you'd probably like to keep out of your pretty little town."

Silas sat back in his chair and propped his feet on his desk. "You're a Darcy. It took me a minute to place you. The accent threw me. I'd heard there was another one of your lot running around."

There was no love lost there, Ciaran thought grimly. Clearly the man's association with Samuel hadn't endeared the rest of the Darcy clan to him. "Some of us are a bit more palatable than others."

"Say what you need to say about Joey, then get the hell out of my office," Silas demanded.

Ciaran made it a point to sit down in the chair across from the desk, even though he hadn't been invited to do so. "Your cousin was cellmates with a nice Russian fellow by the name of Sergei. Sergei, who has since shuffled off this mortal coil, put Joey in touch with some associates of his who are looking to move a very nasty drug into your charming little area...ever heard of Krokodile?"

Silas's expression hardened, his already thin lips disappearing behind his mustache. "I've heard of it. And the little shit knows better."

"He knows better than to handle a firearm as a felon on parole, too," Ciaran reminded him gently.

"I'll talk to him," Silas said. "I don't think Joey would be that stupid, but I'll make damned certain of it."

Ciaran nodded. "While you're at it, make certain that he leaves Harlow Tate in peace. Now that I've been accepted into the clan, I'm feeling very protective."

"What the hell is Harlow Tate to the Darcys?" Barnes demanded.

"Apparently, she's now with Quentin...seems her taste in men has improved significantly. It'd be a shame to have some hot-headed idiot ruin your long-standing relationship with the Darcys, now wouldn't it? Now that Samuel is no longer running the show, the people of Fontaine might not be as forgiving when you turn a blind eye to things."

Ciaran closed the door, but he could hear Barnes cursing him from behind the closed door.

Silas waited half a heartbeat after the newest Darcy left his office before picking up his cell phone again. Discarding the half-written text to the very married hairdresser he'd been fucking for the last few months, he pulled up Joey's number and called him. When the little shit answered, Silas didn't hesitate before chewing him a new asshole.

"What the hell are you into, you stupid little fucker?"

Joey sputtered. "What the fuck, man? You're not my father!"

"No, but I am the sheriff of this town, and if you're bringing in the shit that I think you are, I am gonna put your ass back in prison personally!"

Joey laughed. "The fuck you are. You've been balls deep in the dirty goings on in Fontaine for so long that the dirt on you would fill Commonwealth Stadium! And I know more of it than you think I do."

Silas cursed. "Krokodile, Joey? That shit will tear this town apart!"

"You think I don't know that? But thing is, Silas, these

aren't the kind of people you turn down. They ask you to do something for them, and you do it...otherwise you wind up with a few extra holes in you. And *that's* if you're lucky."

"Promise me you're not bringing that shit to Fontaine...I don't want to have to send you back to prison. It would kill your mama."

"Don't make me play hardball with you, Silas. You're family, but I'll throw you to the damned wolves if I have to."

Silas didn't doubt that for a minute. Joey had no notion of loyalty, that sniveling little shit. It was going to get ugly, and he didn't have any other choice. But...on the upside, he had Harlow Tate handy to take the fall. It wouldn't be too difficult to make her look guilty as sin.

"We need to talk this out face-to-face. I can help get you out of this, if you let me," Silas lied.

Joey scoffed at that. "Yeah, right. There's no way in hell we're getting out of this...me and Tommy are in too deep."

Silas covered his face with his hands. The last thing he needed was for his baby brother to get dragged into this mess. A cousin was one thing, but a sibling was something else altogether. Voters didn't much care for a sheriff with a drug-dealing brother.

"Meet me at the diner on twenty-seven," he said.

"I'll meet you at Mama's," Joey said.

"No. There's a Darcy in town looking for you...he's already been to your mama's once. He'll be watching for you there."

Joey capitulated with a sigh. "Fine. But Silas, I trust you as far as I can throw you...I'll be coming armed."

So would he. "You're family, Joey. Family comes first."

"What the fuck ever, man."

Twelve

Lowey woke up slowly, feeling slightly disoriented. The weight of Quentin's arm draped over her ribs was a little uncomfortable, but she was reluctant to move. He still slept soundly beside her, and for the moment, at least, she wanted to enjoy it.

She didn't trust him. He wasn't the kind who'd stick, and she knew that, but it was nice to lay there next to him and pretend just for a little while. Craning her neck, she looked at him, taking in all the details. He was beat all to hell, but he was still the best-looking man she'd ever seen. Even battered and bruised, that bone structure was perfection. With the perfectly trimmed beard and always meticulously groomed hair, Quentin probably spent more time and effort on his appearance than she did. Not that he needed to. Now, lying there in the bed, his hair mussed, she was seeing something of him that she never had before.

They'd had sex more times and more ways than she could even count, but never once had they slept together.

As if he'd heard her thoughts, his eyes opened slowly. "Stop thinking," he said.

"Not possible," she replied.

"Stop *over*thinking," he retorted.

"That's not possible either," she shot back.

"We're good for right now. You, me. This bed. The pain in my ribs has let up just enough that I think maybe we can have more hot, amazing sex in the next century at least."

A giggle escaped her. Immediately, she clapped her hand over her mouth. Giggling wasn't her. She was not *that* girl. More to the point, she and Quentin were not *that* couple. It was all hot sex with just enough kink to make her blush when she remembered it. Laughing, teasing one another, cuddling in bed—they didn't do that. But it was happening, and God help her, it was more tempting even than his perfect body.

"You're doing it again," he said. "Overthinking."

"Can't help it. You look like Quentin Darcy, but you sure as hell don't act like him."

He rolled her onto her back and settled on top of her, kissing her cheeks, her nose, the line of her jaw. But then his lips settled on her neck, and the sweetness of the moment morphed into something else entirely. Suddenly, it was all heat and need again.

"If you need me to prove that I'm Quentin Darcy," he said, "There's only one way to do that."

"Your pants are a little far away for you to be showing me your driver's license."

He frowned, clearly not appreciating her humor. "I was thinking more along the lines of having someone vouch for me...I thought, if you wanted to go, I'd take you home."

"To your fancy condo?"

"No...to my family's home," he said. "Dinner with Mia and Bennett? Maybe get Clayton and Annalee to come over and bring the munchkin."

Panic. That was the only word to describe what she felt. He wasn't just talking about showing her the house. He was talking about introducing her to his family. Yes, sure, she knew them. Fontaine was the kind of town where everyone knew everyone. But he was staking a claim, he was willing to state openly and to everyone who was important in his life that she was too.

"Slow your roll, Ace," she said. "I don't think that any of us are ready for that."

"I'm not thinking about this stuff anymore, Lowey. I just want to do what feels right."

"And it feels right to you to take me to meet your family?" she demanded.

"It feels right to me to stop hiding the fact that we're together."

Together. That was a loaded statement, she thought. It implied things that she wasn't quite sure he could manage. "But we're not together...not really."

He kissed her again, his beard rasping over her skin in a way that made her shiver. "Meeting my family seems to be a good first step. Come with me, Lowey."

"Jesus! It's like we're in fucking middle school again!"

"When you were in middle school...well, it wouldn't have been illegal, but it would have been seriously questionable for me to be having these kinds of thoughts about you."

She laughed at that, unable to help herself. "If they hate me," she finally managed, "It's on you."

"They won't hate you. Me...I'm not so sure about. I did have an epic redneck brawl on the front lawn Thanksgiving Day. I'm in the doghouse."

She pushed him away and sat up. "If we're going, I need to shower and get ready before I change my mind."

Quentin rolled onto his back and watched her as she moved around the room. It was mundane, really. She gathered clothes from the closet, toiletries from the bag on the dresser. But she was doing it all buck naked, and there was nothing better than watching her move when she didn't have a stitch on.

She glanced over her shoulder at him, saw him watching and made a face. "Pervert."

"Abso-fucking-lutely."

Laughing, he rolled to his side as she tossed a shoe at him. "Be nice," he admonished. "I'm on the injured list."

That prompted an eye roll from her. "Judging by our earlier activities, you're not that injured."

"Oh, I am," he said. "But with the right incentive, I can power through."

"And on that note, I'm getting in the shower." She paused, looking back at him, and added, "Alone."

He was still chuckling as she closed the bathroom door firmly behind her. Sitting up, he winced as his ribs reminded him just how hard his half brother could punch and reached for his discarded pants. After digging his cell from the pocket, he started to text Mia. They hadn't spoken since he'd Jerry Springer-ed her Thanksgiving. Deciding that a phone call and a well-timed apology were more likely to get him what he wanted, he dialed her number instead.

She answered quickly, and her response was pretty much as expected. "You're an asshole," she said flatly.

"We are in total agreement," he offered. "I'm sorry I ruined your big holiday plans. It was a dick move."

Her heavy sigh was all he needed. She'd forgive him. Mia's downfall was that she was always too forgiving. At least it worked in his favor.

"What do you want, Quentin? You wouldn't be calling and apologizing if there wasn't something in it for you."

The truth hurts, he thought. "I do...but it's fairly benign."

"Spill it, big brother."

Quentin took a breath, glanced at the bathroom door, and then said something he'd never thought to utter. "I want to bring Lowey to the house for dinner...and if you're not doing anything with it, I want to get Grandma's ring from Mama's jewelry box."

Mia had been half listening to her brother, assuming he was just trying to con her into forgetting his bad behavior. She'd been watching through the back window as Bennett cleared brush in the backyard. It was the end of November but unseasonably warm, and he'd worked up a sweat while wearing nothing but jeans and a white T-shirt. Maybe that was why it took her a second to process what Quentin had just said because her ovaries had temporarily shut down higher brain function.

When it did register, she turned away from the window and sank down onto the nearest horizontal surface. "You serious?"

"As a heart attack," Quentin replied.

Mia felt a little breathless at the thought. Quentin

didn't talk to her. Not about things that mattered. In fact, as far as she knew, he didn't talk to anyone about things that mattered. He kept it all bottled up inside him, like any softer emotion was a crime to be concealed. "You want to marry her?"

"Not tomorrow," he snapped. "But when all this business is settled with Joey Barnes, when there's time for us to sit and talk about everything, then I'm going to ask her."

"Don't wait until things are settled." If there was one thing Mia had learned in her life, waiting for things to be right was pointless. If he loved Harlow Tate, and she had to believe he did because Quentin was the most commitment-phobic person on the planet, he needed to move on it and not waste another second. "If you love her, and if you want to be with her, just do it. Don't let anyone or anything stop you."

There was silence on the line for the longest time, until he finally spoke again. "I'm sorry, Mia. We should have done something about Samuel...long before now. If I'd known—"

"You'd have killed him. Your temper still isn't the best, especially where he's concerned," she stated. "This is how it was supposed to be. If I'd run off with Bennett when we were younger, I don't know what would have happened. Maybe we could have made it work, maybe not. But what I do know is that living the last ten years without him gave me enough time to realize just how special it is. I appreciate having him in my life now in a way that I might not have before."

It was true, she realized. She'd had to let him go to understand just how much he meant to her, how vital he was to her life and her happiness. Did Harlow Tate make Quentin feel that way? God, she hoped so. He needed some happiness in his life. He needed some peace from whatever it was that haunted him so much.

"Dinner won't be fancy," she said. "But it'll be ready at seven. You want Clayton and Annalee here to witness your taming?"

His bark of laughter made her smile. Quentin didn't do that nearly enough.

"I'll never be tamed, Mia," he scoffed.

"So you say." She laughed. "But I've seen Harlow Tate, Quentin. I know just what that girl looks like, and I know just how little of your crap she'll tolerate. You might not be completely tamed, but you'll definitely be domesticated under the right circumstances."

He changed the subject then. "Lowey is getting out of the shower. I'll see you tonight."

The call ended abruptly, leaving Mia sitting there holding the phone and shaking her head in wonder. If any woman could ever bring Quentin to heel, it would be Harlow Tate, and she was eager to see it.

The back door slammed, and she looked up to see Bennett walking in, stripping off his sweaty shirt and looking like every erotic fantasy she'd had for the last decade.

"You keep looking at me like that," he warned, "And I'm not going to be responsible for my actions."

She dropped the phone onto the couch beside her and leaned back, resting her weight on her palms. "Is that a promise or a threat?"

Bennett stalked toward her until he could tangle his hands in her hair. Then he kissed her, his lips firm on hers. It was definitely a promise, she decided. When the kiss broke, she was breathless. "I should be getting everything ready for dinner tonight...we're having guests."

"We'll order pizza," he offered.

"No," she said. "We will not. But since it's warm enough outside, there's no reason you couldn't fire up the grill and cook some steaks. That might free up a little bit of time this afternoon."

Bennett grinned and then scooped her up, draping her over his shoulder as he made his way toward the stairs. They were halfway to the landing when the sound of breaking glass stopped them cold.

"Put me down," Mia said, but Bennett was already lowering her to her feet.

"I'll go check it out," he offered.

"No," she said. "That came from Mama's room!"

She was already rushing past him, toward the former library that had been modified for Patricia. But inside the door, she stopped abruptly. There was no one there except her mother. Patricia lay in the bed, motionless as always. But the lamp beside her bed was broken on the floor, and the cord dangled from her fingertips.

"What is happening here?" she asked, terrified to even hope.

Bennett shook his head. "I wish to hell I knew, baby. I wish I knew."

Thirteen

Quentin parked the car in front of the house and noted that Clayton and Annalee were already there. He smiled, looking forward to seeing Emma Grace. His only niece was shamelessly spoiled but still a sweet kid, and he enjoyed her tremendously.

Getting out of the car he walked around to open Lowey's door for her. He could smell the fired-up grill, and his stomach rumbled.

"Oh my god!" Lowey said. "That smells amazing...and I'm starving."

"We did skip lunch," he pointed out. He'd talked her back into bed with him, and it had been amazing.

"Yes, we did. Because you whined like a little bitch until I agreed to have sex with you again."

He took her hand, lacing his fingers through hers. "Whatever works." Her answering giggle was a very un-Lowey-like sound. She tried so hard to be stoic all the time, to be tough as nails, and to never let anyone see the softer side of her, the sweetness under the salt.

"Thank you," he added.

"What for?"

"For coming here with me...for letting me show everyone that you're special, that you're different, and that somehow I'm different with you."

She stopped then, blinking at him, her lips parted in a soft O. "You gotta stop saying things like that to me...if you're playing me, Quent—"

"I'm not playing you, Lowey. Playing you was never my intent. I just never expected to have these feelings...not for you or for anyone."

"Why do you close yourself off so much?" she asked. "I know why I do it, but you seemed to grow up in the perfect family."

He laughed bitterly. "Not perfect...about as far from it as possible. Living with Samuel Darcy was like lighting matches while sitting on top of a powder keg. You knew it was gonna go off, just not *when*."

Recalling the fights, the blow-ups, the endless stream of disapproval where nothing any of them ever did was good enough for Samuel, he wondered how any of them could have been even remotely functional as adults. But, in retrospect Quentin realized, he'd borne the brunt of it.

Clayton had been good at everything, excelling at sports, at academics. Mia had been an angel, right up until Bennett Hayes came along. But him? He'd been the troublemaker, always getting into fights, getting into trouble, ready to swing his fists at the drop of a hat. He couldn't count the number of times that Samuel had told him how unlovable he was, how worthless he was, and that he would never amount to anything.

But Patricia had always been there, always available to hug him and to tell him that he was worth something. "Mom made it bearable," he admitted, "But Samuel...he's a real piece of work, that son of a bitch. Cold through to the bone."

"I wish I'd known her better," Lowey said softly, as they paused on the steps of the porch. "What I did know of her was pretty damned impressive."

"I wish you could have too," he agreed, and then crossed the porch to knock on the door. "Come on. Let's get in here so my siblings can bust my balls, and you can enjoy watching someone else abuse me for a change."

Silas had taken a car from the impound lot, one that wouldn't be missed and that wouldn't draw notice. The compact was just about as nondescript as a car could be. He let himself into The Kicking Mule and helped himself to one of the guns Lowey kept stashed under the counter. It hadn't been difficult. The place was shot all to hell, thanks to his asshole cousin. The door was barely on the hinges after all that.

When Joey's truck pulled into the parking lot, Silas braced himself for what he was going to have to do. He didn't take it lightly. The Barnes clan was as dysfunctional as one family could be, but blood was blood, and the idea of having to take out one of his own didn't sit well with him. But if he'd learned one thing in his years of having Samuel Darcy on his back like he was in a goddamn harness, you did what was necessary to save yourself.

As Joey got out and crossed the parking lot of the nearly deserted café, Silas turned the key in the ignition to start the engine. Joey climbed in, and Silas nodded. "We need to go someplace a little more private...I didn't think there'd be so many people still here."

Joey eyed the thinning crowd. "There's all of five people here, Si, and most of them are so damned old they can't see five feet in front of 'em much less across the parking lot."

Silas ignored the complaints and turned the car back onto the highway. "You may not have a reputation to protect in this town, but I do. I still need these asshats to vote for me."

Joey's eye roll spoke volumes. "You could be raking in a fortune if you wanted to, but you're still too worried about what people think of you."

And that was the difference between them. All Joey could see was getting rich quick. Silas knew that he'd get more in the long run by playing his cards right and angling for higher offices. That meant damage control by any means necessary.

Taking the highway out of town and toward Fire Creek, Silas slowed when he reached the turn-off for the abandoned house. He had the gun in his hand before the car even came to a full stop.

"Get out of the car, Joey," he said.

"What the fuck are you doing?"

Silas shook his head. "You're making problems. Bigger problems than I can afford to handle. You bring those drugs into this town, and any shot I have at becoming a senator are long gone."

"It's too fucking late for that," Joey said. "They're already here...we've already got the distribution set up! These guys get disappointed, and no one in this town is going to be safe!"

"That's a chance I'll have to take," Silas replied. "But the bottom line is, you're a threat to me, Joey...a threat to my future goals. You're more valuable to me as a tragic casualty of domestic violence...you'll go from being a liability to being a platform."

"Then shoot me in this fucking car if you're going to because I'm not getting out and making it easy for you," Joey said.

Before Silas could react, Joey lunged at him. They struggled, both of them grappling for control of the weapon. Silas cursed, gritting his teeth as he tried to keep the younger man from twisting the pistol from his grasp. Just when he thought it was over, when he thought Joey had won, his cousin's finger slipped on the trigger.

The sound was deafening in the car, but it was the smell that hit him instantly. The faint burning smell and the coppery aroma of blood mingled sickeningly in the small space.

Joey gasped, his mouth working as blood bubbled from between his parted lips. It wasn't the first time Silas had watched someone die. Hell, it wasn't even the first time he'd watched someone die by his own hand. But it was the first time that he'd killed someone he'd taken care of as a child, someone whose funeral he'd have to attend as one of the bereaved.

Climbing out of the car, he walked around to the passenger side and opened the door. Dragging Joey's still warm but lifeless body out of the vehicle, he concealed it in the trees. All that was left was to clean the car, return it to impound and burn his clothes. The gun would go back to The Kicking Mule, and when Joey was reported missing, his body would be found after an appropriately difficult search and questioning his ex-wife, with their long history of bad blood, would be the only logical option.

Fourteen

They didn't eat in the dining room, and no one dressed for dinner. All her Downton Abbey-esque visions of the grandeur of being a Darcy were dashed as they huddled around the kitchen island eating burgers and drinking beer straight from the bottles. Lowey watched them for a moment, taking in the easy way they all talked with one another, the comfort and camaraderie they had with one another.

She'd never had that, she realized. Not with anyone in her life had she ever been so at ease. The closest she'd come to that was with Quentin, but still, it was a revelation to see him in this light. Good natured, charming, as close to being at peace as she'd ever witnessed him.

"So, tell me, Lowey, have you hired a contractor to patch up the bar yet?"

The question had come from Bennett. "No, not yet. Until the insurance adjuster gets back to me, I won't really know if that's even feasible. It's a lot of damage, and I'm fairly certain I am underinsured," she answered.

"It'll be all right," he said. "I can drag Carter down

there, and we'll help you put it right. We work for beer, too."

"It will be put back together," Quentin promised. "I'll help, too. Even if it does mean hanging out with two Hayeses. Double the fun. Yay."

Mia flicked a plastic fork in Quentin's direction. "Be nice, or you'll pay for it." Bennett laughed, but she tossed a glare at him. "You too. I'm done with people in this family fighting and carrying on with each other and with the rest of the world...and FYI, Quentin, I invited Ciaran tonight, but he couldn't make it. The next time you two are in a room together, if there's any blood spilled, I will skin you both. Is that clear?"

Lowey watched Quentin duck his head to hide his grin as he muttered, "Yes, ma'am."

When he glanced over at her, she saw it in him—the darkness that was simply a part of him. He was in his element here, laughing and joking with his family, to the point that she was keenly aware of the fact that she was an outsider. But with that little glimpse, she realized something else, something far more important than the fact that she didn't quite fit in with the whole Darcy crowd. There was a part of him that only she knew, a part of him that no one else would ever see.

It set her at ease, seeing that in him. It gave her a sense of relief because in that moment, she knew that whether or not she belonged with *them*, she still belonged with *him*.

He moved closer to her, leaning down to whisper against her ear. "You okay?"

"I am now," she answered. "How are you? Ribs hurting?"

"Only when I laugh. Or breathe. Or move. Or think... but I'm good. Another beer, and I'll be amazing, in fact."

"Have all you want. I'll drive us home...I could get used to touring around in your baby."

"Whoa...hold up. He let you drive his car?" Clayton demanded, gaping at them both. "I'm his goddamn *brother,* and he won't let me drive it!"

"Yes, but I have boobs," Lowey answered.

"They do provide a lot of opportunity, don't they?" Annalee observed. "Now close your mouth, Clayton."

"On a more serious note and while we're all here together," Mia said, "We need to talk about Mama."

Lowey was still looking up at him. She could see the muscle ticking in his jaw, could feel the tension that flooded him. It rolled off him in waves, and she sat back, waiting for the explosion.

Quentin tamped down the spark of hope, beat it down as brutally as Ciaran had beaten him. "There's nothing to talk about, Mia," he said. "Nothing has changed, and nothing is ever going to change. We just have to accept it and make the best of it."

"But there *is* something to talk about, Quentin. And things are changing. There have been little signs, moments and glimpses where I could swear she's right there with us...and then today—"

She stopped abruptly, her lips trembling as she tried to regain her composure. He hated seeing that, hated seeing the hope that would only be dashed again. He knew that feeling, that dark and empty hole that just sucked you into it every time. "Don't do this to yourself, Mia. There's no percentage in it. If wishful thinking could cure her, she'd have been dancing a jig years ago!"

"She knocked a lamp over today," Mia stated softly.

"Bullshit. It fell," he countermanded. It wasn't possible. There was no way in hell it was possible.

"It happened, Quentin," she insisted. "Bennett and I were both on the stairs, and we heard it. When we went into her room to check, she was lying there in the bed, with the cord between her fingers, and for just a second...I swear she was looking at me. *She was seeing me, Quentin.*"

He could feel the air being sucked right out of his lungs. It was like Thanksgiving all over again. She'd been there. He'd felt her presence, if that was even possible. It was almost like being haunted by a woman who was still living.

"Mia, this sounds completely crazy," he protested. He couldn't let himself believe it. None of them would survive the heartbreak and disappointment.

"There have been subtle changes," Annalee insisted. "I've seen them. Movements, albeit small ones, especially of her facial muscles. I don't know the extent of the damage from the head injury...none of us do. But I have been reading up on something called Locked-In Syndrome. And I think before you all make any decisions about Patricia's care, you need to consider that as an option."

Clayton was saying nothing, hanging back, weighing the options as always. After several minutes of silence, a silence that seemed to stretch on forever, he finally spoke. "We'll get the best doctors. We'll have her re-evaluated and see if there's any change in her brain activity...I've had my own experiences in the last month or so. There has been a moment or two where I thought—well, that doesn't matter. Right now, we put it in the hands of the doctors and let them point us in the right direction."

"I still say it's bullshit," Quentin protested. "We're

seeing what we want to, and that's all." He couldn't afford to let himself believe otherwise, even if the rest of the family had put on their rose-colored glasses. And he needed to go. He needed to get out before he lost it altogether.

Turning to Lowey, he said, "I'm ready to go if you are."

"Sure," she agreed before turning to Mia, "Thank you for dinner. It was a nice evening."

"We'll do it again soon," Mia replied. "When someone gets his panties untwisted."

Quentin flipped her the bird as they walked out into the night.

Fifteen

Ciaran rolled over in bed and ran his hand over the soft curve of Loralei's hip. As he reached the tiny elastic band and began to slip his fingers beneath it, she gripped his wrist and pushed him away.

He sighed heavily. "I'd ask if you're still mad, but I think you've made it abundantly clear."

She glanced over her shoulder at him. "Our first event with your family...the family you traveled halfway around the world to find! And you had to beat your half brother nearly to death in the front yard?"

Ciaran offered her an innocent expression. "I didn't beat him that badly, love. Just worked him over a little bit...don't be mad, love. Or be mad...and we can fight and make up."

"You've only got one person to make up with, and it's not me," she replied firmly.

"I'm making amends!" he protested. "I'm helping him with his girl, aren't I?"

"Only because it benefits you!"

"Us!"

"He's your brother!"

Ciaran sighed and rolled onto his back. "I'm not doing it strictly because of the Russians. I'd have helped him regardless of Barnes's connection to them. And in spite of handing him his ass, I like the bastard!"

Loralei rolled over and gaped at him. "You have a funny way of showing it."

"There's a pecking order in every family, love. In every clan, gang, or squad...there's always a pecking order. I had to show that I don't need them, and that I'm not going to be forever standing in the doorway with my hat in my hands like Oliver fucking Twist...that's all it was. He'll recover, and we'll have a healthy respect for one another in the end."

She scooted closer to him then. "That's all it is? Just he-man, macho, alpha male bullshit?"

"We're crude creatures, love. We like to blow things up, beat on each other, and then drink...it's the manly way."

He could tell she was softening toward him a little. Her body had relaxed, and he could feel the weight of her breasts pressing against him. If he could just get her to laugh, then they'd be back on track.

Before he could even figure out how to do that, his cell phone buzzed from the nightstand. Cursing under his breath, he looked at the screen. It was Matt, Loralei's brother, and that was not a good sign.

"What is it?" he asked and then listened silently before ending the call and climbing out of bed. As he reached for his pants, he looked back at Loralei. "I'm going to have to weasel my way back into your good graces later. Joey Barnes's body was just found by a bunch of drunk high school kids."

Loralei sat up. "His body?"

"Someone shot him in the gut," Ciaran replied. "And Silas Barnes is on his way to question Harlow Tate...one of the deputies, who isn't completely crooked, tipped Matt off. He means to have her arrested for this whether she did it or not."

"I'm coming with you," she said.

"Don't," he replied. "I have no idea what's going to happen, and you may need to work on getting bail money together for her. I don't doubt for a second that Silas will be able to manufacture enough cause for an arrest, even if he has to plant it himself."

"But she was with Quentin all along, right?"

Ciaran shook his head. "Any decent lawyer will be able to discredit her lover as an alibi...we can only hope that Joey was still alive at the time they showed up at Mia's. If not, if Quentin is her only alibi, and Silas Barnes is determined to pin this on her...she'll get off eventually, but it won't be easy. He'll fight it every step of the way."

"I'll talk to Kaitlyn about bail money. I don't have it myself, but she does, and I know she'll help out if I ask her to."

"I shouldn't put that on you," he said. "This is my fucked-up family after all...the thing is, I know how much money they've poured into the distillery, Lor. And Quentin could probably get her out of jail, but it would take every dime he's got."

"I don't mind," Loralei replied. "I like Lowey. I've always liked Lowey, and I know just what a shit Silas Barnes can be. Any Barnes for that matter. It's just a whole freaking barrel full of bad apples."

Ciaran kissed her soundly on the lips, but it was more an expression of affection and gratitude than the wicked things that had been on his mind earlier. "I do love you,

Loralei Elizabeth Crawford. And even if this all comes to naught, I do appreciate what you've done to try and give me the family I wanted...and if it doesn't work, you're all I ever needed anyway."

She blinked at him as tears filled her eyes. "Damn you, Ciaran! I wanted to be mad at you for a little longer."

He was smiling and whistling as he walked out the door.

Lowey was standing at the counter in the kitchen of the small carriage house. A glance at the clock told her it was nearly three in the morning. Quentin was in bed, but she'd been unable to sleep. Rather than stare up at the ceiling, she'd gotten up. She was worried about so many things—the bar was her home and her livelihood. Her savings account wouldn't carry her forever. Hell, she'd be lucky if it carried her through Christmas. But that wasn't what kept her awake. It was him. She was worried he would break her heart all over again, and she also worried because, in that moment, her heart was breaking for him.

Quentin had been quiet since they'd left Mia's, and she knew that the conversation about his mother was weighing on him. He was afraid to hope, and she understood that perhaps better than anyone. Being afraid to believe that any positive sign wasn't just too good to be true was an all too familiar sensation for her.

In fact, she'd been having that same feeling since he'd walked into her bar not even two days ago. Had it really been less than forty-eight hours since her life and her heart had been turned upside down all over again?

"Nothing will ever fuck you up as bad as that man,

Lowey. Nothing," she muttered to herself as she opened the refrigerator and retrieved a bottle of water from inside. She didn't know who'd come in and stocked it for them, but the gift basket of fruit and other goodies on the counter had been very welcome.

The bedroom door opened, and she looked up to see Quentin standing there. Shirtless, his jeans half undone, hair mussed, God above, he was hot.

"I'm sorry I dragged you out the way I did," he offered. "I let it get to me, and you paid for it. As usual."

She rolled her eyes. "Leaving early wasn't quite the hardship you make it out to be. I like your family. They're nice people. Welcoming and warm...but I don't belong there."

It was his turn to roll his eyes, and he did. "Do not start that shit again. You're as good as anyone else!"

"Yes, I am. But as good as and same as are very different things," she explained. "I will never be the kind of woman you can take to dinners or fundraisers. I will never be a soccer mom like Annalee, even assuming you and I would manage to avoid killing each other long enough to get married and have kids...hell, we've never even talked about whether or not either of us wants kids!"

"Since you're predicting gloom and doom in our relationship, why not branch out a little? What day will I die? What horrible illness or accident will have me meeting my maker?" he demanded. "Jesus, Lowey! Can we not just *be*? I want you in my life...I don't know about forever, and I don't know about kids. And if I wanted a soccer mom, there are about fifteen single ones in this town who've been knocking on my door since you and I split up."

That brought her up short. "And I just bet you let them in, didn't you?"

He ran his hands through his hair. "No, dammit. I

didn't. I haven't been with another woman since you...I haven't wanted to, and that's the hell of it."

"I find that difficult to believe," she snapped.

He walked toward her, that slow easy stride that had all his muscles rippling and her heart pounding. Just inches separated them when he stopped, close enough that she could feel the heat of him. "Doesn't matter whether you believe it or not, Lowey. I said it because it's the truth, not because I'm trying to convince you of anything."

"Quentin, we're fooling ourselves if either of us expects this thing to work. You do know that, right?"

"No," he said. "I don't. I've always said I wasn't good at commitment, but the simple truth is, I've never tried. I've never met anyone who made me want to."

"Quentin—"

"*Harlow*," he interrupted. "Just stop...stop putting up roadblocks. Stop looking for ways out when we aren't even *in* yet."

She was doing exactly that, and she was ballsy enough to admit it to herself, if not to him. But that didn't mean she was wrong to do it. Neither of them had great track records. He was right when he'd said he'd never tried commitment. Quentin Darcy was the ultimate playboy. Rich, good looking, always up for a good time but never one to stick around too long. He'd had a reputation for being the love 'em and leave 'em king.

As for her, it was like she'd made a habit of finding every man in a tri-county radius that she shouldn't be with and was slowly making her way down the list.

"Just don't break my heart," she said. "Seriously, Quentin. Don't do it. I'll make you regret it."

He grinned at that, and it was so devastatingly sexy, she wanted to climb him right there on the spot. "Why don't you take me to bed and help me stop overthinking everything for a while?"

"I don't need to take you to bed for that," he said and stepped closer, backing her against the counter. His hand slipped easily into her hair, tugging it just a shade less than gently. It was all the incentive she needed. Hooking her fingers beneath the waistband of his jeans, she tugged him closer still.

"Just how naughty should we be in someone else's kitchen?" she asked.

"As naughty as we want to be," he replied smoothly as he lifted her onto the counter.

It was the most natural thing in the world to part her knees and cradle him between her thighs. Even then, she wanted more. She wanted him so close that not even air would exist between them. With that in mind, she reached for the zipper of his jeans, sliding it down with slow and deliberate movements.

"You're rushing," he said as he kissed the side of her neck, then followed it with a stinging nip.

"Do you want me to slow down?" she asked, sliding her hand inside his pants, cupping her hand around his hardening cock. "I can stop altogether if you want."

"No," he replied breathlessly. "Don't ever stop."

Stroking him, alternating the pressure by gently touching him or closing her fingers firmly around him, she reveled in his response to her. It didn't hurt that the entire time she was teasing him to a fever pitch, he was doing the same to her. His hands were never still. They roamed over her body, and his mouth followed suit. When he closed his lips around one taut nipple, still covered by the layers of her clothes, she let her head fall back and savored the sensation.

"God, you drive me crazy," she said on a harsh breath.

He gripped the hem of her sweater, tugging it up and over her head before cupping her breasts in his hands, kneading them gently as his thumbs played her nipples expertly. God, he knew just how to touch her.

Lowey shoved his jeans and the boxers beneath them down over his hips before taking him completely in her hand. Closing her fingers around him, she stroked him firmly at the base of his shaft, gentling her touch as she reached the head. Running her thumb over the glistening crown, she smiled when he bit out a curse word.

"Dammit, Lowey," he whispered harshly. "If you want this to last more than sixty seconds, you're gonna have to ease up. A man can only take so much."

"Stop talking and just fuck me," she urged. "I don't want to think or worry. I just want to feel good for as long as I can."

Sixteen

Quentin was so far gone he couldn't even tell which way was up. With her perched on the edge of the counter, her long legs locked around him, and her soft hand stroking his cock, it was a wonder he could string two words together much less say anything important. But he needed to tell her. The words had been pressing on him for so long that it would be a relief to finally just have them out there.

"Jesus, Lowey," he muttered as she circled him with her thumb. She could tempt a saint, and he'd never been accused of being that. It took all his willpower to reach down and grasp her wrist, stilling her hand. "We need to talk, whether you want to or not."

"Nothing good ever begins with the phrase 'we need to talk.' Nothing."

He grinned at that. "Normally, I'd agree with you... but I don't think this is bad. I hope to hell you don't either."

She leaned back, her palms flat on the counter to support her weight. It was sexy as hell, but he didn't think for one minute that she was trying to be. That was the hell of it with Lowey. Everything she did was unconsciously, innately sensual.

"What do you want to talk about?" she asked softly, and there was no mistaking the trepidation in her voice.

"I think I love you," he said. In his head, he'd prepared a great speech, but there in the moment, it was gone. Instead, the words just tumbled out and landed like a bomb between them.

She blinked at him for a second. "That is not what I expected you to say."

"What were you expecting?"

She shrugged. "That what we have is great, but that we're getting ahead of ourselves, that we should still see other people, that it's not me, it's you. The list is endless, but you saying you thought you loved me wasn't anywhere on it."

"You had to know that...you had to know that if I can't walk away from you, there's a reason. What other reason could it be?" he asked.

"I don't know. I didn't know why you walked away two months ago, and I didn't know why you walked back into my bar yesterday," she admitted. "What you just said to me, Quentin, it's what I needed to hear from you two months ago."

The implication that despite everything that had passed between them, it was too late, was there. And maybe she was right. Maybe it was too late. Maybe his fear of commitment, his fear of opening up and letting anyone in, had already wrecked what was probably the best thing that had ever happened in his life. But he had to try. If the last two months had been any indication, whatever hurt pride or hurt feelings he was risking by laying it on the line couldn't be any worse than the misery of being without her and wondering *what if*.

"Then let me rephrase. I don't think that I'm in love with you, Harlow. I *know* I am. And as much of an ass as it makes me to admit it, I walked out on you because I was too much of a coward to face it then."

She let her head fall back and sighed up to the ceiling. "And when you get spooked again? What happens then, Quentin? I'm fine with us this way...you and me, and whatever happens just happens. No promises mean no expectations...but if you promise me things, if you let me hope for things, and then you take it away—I don't know if I can forgive that."

"I'm sticking this time, Lowey. Whatever it takes. You can count on it."

"I want so badly to believe that," she whispered.

"If you let me, I'll prove it," he promised. He leaned in and pressed a kiss to the hollow of her throat, then traced his tongue over the arch of her collarbone. "Starting now."

Quentin reached for the button of her jeans and freed it with a flick of his thumb before sliding the zipper down. Tugging them over her hips, he dropped them onto the floor and then pressed her back onto the countertop. He let his hands roam over her, touching her everywhere, savoring every shudder and moan from her.

With Lowey, it wasn't just about his own pleasure and making her come had nothing to do with his own ego. It went beyond that, to something deep and visceral. Primal even. She was *his*. In every way that mattered, and whether she stayed with him or not, this part of her would be his forever. Maybe it was ego, after all, because he wanted her to feel that. He wanted to know that long after he was gone, she'd still bear his mark on a part of her that no one else would ever touch.

Quentin kissed her again, taking her mouth, staking a claim. And then he moved lower, trailing kisses along her neck, her breasts, pausing to tease each nipple. Just as he reached the band of her underwear, a loud and obnoxious bang sounded at the door.

"You have got to be fucking kidding me," he muttered and rested his head against her hip for just a second. "Who the fuck would be looking for us here?"

"Ciaran," she said. "Or one of your other siblings... they're the only ones who know where we are. Whoever it is, they have shitty timing."

He pulled his pants up and then gathered her discarded clothing. "Epically shitty...but this—this is not done. The minute we get rid of them, I'm going to lick every fucking inch of you."

"Well, that's romantic."

"It will be," he said. "And if it isn't, it's going to feel so damn good you won't care."

He walked toward the door, but stood there, waiting until Lowey was fully dressed again to open it. The pounding resumed along with a booming announcement.

"It's the Sheriff! I know you're in there, and you need to open up the door immediately."

Quentin glanced back at Lowey. "This can't be good."

"It never is. But let the son of a bitch in."

Quentin opened the door to see Silas standing there accompanied by two Fayette County officers. He was out of his jurisdiction since Ash Grove Farm was over the county line.

"Silas, you're an unexpected and unwelcome surprise."

"Can the attitude, Darcy," Silas said. "I'm here to serve a warrant."

"For?" Quentin demanded.

"The warrant is issued to my cousin-in-law, not you."

"Former cousin-in-law," Lowey corrected as she stepped forward. She accepted the paperwork from Silas and frowned as she read through it. "Why are you searching The Kicking Mule? There's not enough left of it to hide anything."

"We're looking for a weapon...a handgun in particular. It seems someone shot Joey this evening."

Quentin frowned as Lowey asked. "Is he okay?"

"Why the hell would you care?" Silas demanded.

"For Joey, I don't. But Juanita loves his worthless ass, and that woman has enough misery in her life already," Lowey snapped at him.

"No. He's not okay. He's dead, and frankly no one has more cause to want him that way than you do," Silas replied. "I wouldn't advise taking any trips, Harlow. We're going to want to talk to you again."

"You've served your warrant," Quentin said. "Now get the hell out."

Silas lifted his chin challengingly. "You might run Fontaine, Quentin, but you don't run me. I'm here in an official capacity."

"Which has been completed, and now you can go. Any time." Quentin looked at the officers with him. "Unless there's something else, gentlemen?"

The officers looked at one another, and then one of them looked at Silas. "We're done here, Sheriff Barnes."

After they left, Lowey cursed. "Son of a bitch. We

need to get to the bar. I know there's not much left of it, but what is left will be torn all to hell if Silas has his way."

"How many guns do you have in the bar, Lowey?"

"I've got Papaw's shotgun, and I've got a forty-five stashed there as well. Why?"

"Do you trust Silas to do an honest search? Do you think he's above planting evidence?"

Her face paled. "Let's get to the bar. *Now.*"

Seventeen

Ciaran went straight to The Kicking Mule. He'd texted Quentin and knew that was where they were going. Matt had given him a heads-up that Joey had missed an important meeting with the suppliers. Without seeing the transactions go down, Matt was stuck. He couldn't arrest them simply for being present, which meant he'd have to lean on the cousin, Tommy, get him to step up and take over as point man so they could finally put an end to all of this. He knew Matt had planned to use the threat of a return to prison to bring Joey to heel, but that wouldn't work with Tommy. Of course, Tommy also wasn't nearly the hard ass that Joey was, so it might work still.

In the meantime, Ciaran had his own suspicions about Joey's death. Silas was a man with his eye fixed firmly on the prize. His current position was nothing more than a stepping stone to bigger, better, and more lucrative things. A power-hungry politician with a liability like a relative of Joey's ilk was a recipe for disaster. And Lowey was the perfect scapegoat.

Easing his truck into the parking lot of the bar, he noted the two sheriff's vehicles present. He could hear the breaking of glass and smashing of furniture from inside. He could also hear Quentin yelling.

He acted quickly, crossing the gravel lot at a run and entering the bar. "You've a search warrant for a gun," Ciaran said. "You'll not find it hiding in the bottom of a clear vodka bottle. Smashing it is willful destruction of property—with witnesses!"

The deputy tossed the bottle to the floor, glass and liquor scattering as it shattered. "It slipped."

Ciaran looked back at Lowey who stood there with her lips clamped firmly together and an expression of pure hatred burning in her eyes.

"It can all be replaced," he offered.

"No. It can't. And I'm not even sure I want it to be," she said. "Maybe this is what I needed to push me out of the bar business after all."

One of the deputies reached beneath the bar and retrieved a wooden box. Opening it, he removed the handgun from inside it. "Looks like we've found our weapon."

"You've found *a* weapon," Quentin stated, "Not *the* weapon."

The deputy, one of Silas's brown-nosing sycophants, grinned. "If it walks like a duck and quacks like a duck... where were you this afternoon, Miss Tate?"

"I was with Quentin at Ash Grove Farm," she replied. "And then at around five, we went to have dinner with his siblings at Mia's home."

"There are witnesses who can corroborate that?"

The question had come from Silas who'd just walked into the bar behind Ciaran.

"Mia Darcy, Bennett Hayes, Clayton and Annalee Darcy were all there," Lowey replied. Her tone was robotic, without any inflection at all, as if she'd gotten so used to Silas's accusations and harassment that it no longer registered.

Ciaran didn't point out that he'd been invited to the fête and elected not to go. The object was to remove Lowey from the suspect list, not to put himself on it. But he did watch Silas closely for a reaction, and he wasn't disappointed. The man's face paled, and his breath quickened. He was scared, Ciaran realized, and guilty. Very, *very* guilty.

"Did the kids who found the body see any vehicles near there? Were any tire tracks found?" Ciaran demanded.

Silas turned on him then. "You might be Matt Crawford's errand boy, but that doesn't give you any jurisdiction here."

Ciaran walked over to him, met Silas's guilty gaze directly and warned. "If you don't dot every I and cross every T on this, you'll regret it, Barnes."

"Are you threatening an officer of the law?"

Ciaran smiled. "Only with legal action. You are an elected official, and any elected official can be recalled... especially if there are concerns of corruption and miscarriages of justice."

"You might want to take a step back. This isn't a John Grisham novel," Silas replied. "And bringing yourself to the attention of law enforcement and immigration might not be to your advantage."

Quentin stepped in then. "Correct me if I'm wrong, but I was under the impression that since his father is a citizen, Ciaran's kind of good there. But maybe you need to consult John Grisham on that."

Silas flushed angrily. "I can arrest you for obstruction, Darcy. Don't think I won't."

"You've found what you were looking for," Lowey said. "And you've destroyed everything that was left intact in this bar after your cousin opened fire on it. So, just go, Silas. Take what you came for and go."

Ciaran's lips firmed as he watched Silas's expression turn smug. God, he hated that bastard and what he was doing to her and to Quentin. Sure, he and Quentin had their issues, but he respected him at least. At some point or other, he hoped they'd be able to at least be civil to one another. But their strange-ass family situation aside, what Silas was doing was wrong, plain and simple. The son of a bitch was railroading a woman who was innocent, whose only real crime was to have the unfortunate luck of having been married to Silas's bastard of a cousin.

"I'll go because I'm ready to, not because you demanded it."

Ciaran wanted more than anything to tell him it didn't matter why the hell he left, so long as he did. But saying anything would just escalate the situation and keep Silas trying to come out on top. So, he bit his tongue and watched the asshole walk out, taking his minions with him.

When he was gone, Quentin turned to Ciaran and said, "The only way she's getting out of this is to figure out who did kill Joey Barnes."

"That's an easy enough question to answer," Ciaran said. "Silas killed him."

"What about the Russian drug dealers?" Lowey asked.

"They were waiting for him to show up," Ciaran replied. "And when he didn't, Matt's whole case went south. He can't arrest someone for trafficking if they don't actually ever receive the trafficked goods...Silas is a man with political aspirations. When I told him what his cousin was up to, he saw that political career going up in smoke and decided to do whatever was necessary to prevent it."

Quentin shook his head. "That's a pretty big damn leap there, Sherlock. How exactly, if you're right, do we prove that?"

"*We* don't," Ciaran replied. "*I* do. In the meantime, you all put together a timeline of your whereabouts and anyone who can verify it. You're going to need it."

Lowey looked scared while Quentin just looked pissed off. He wanted to tell them not to worry, but the truth of the matter was they needed to. Silas had the tools at his disposal to make this very ugly, and he was highly motivated to do it.

"Right," Ciaran muttered. "I'm out. I'll work on what I can. You two...just stay the hell out of trouble for a change, will you?" Ciaran turned and headed for the door. His only remaining option was to lean on Silas, and for that, he'd need to do some digging.

Eighteen

Lowey sat down in one of the few remaining chairs. Half of them were broken, the other half were turned over on the floor, the cushions slashed by overzealous deputies on a witch hunt.

"He's going to arrest me, isn't he?" She wanted Quentin to lie to her, but she knew he wouldn't.

"He's going to try," he said. "But I'll do whatever it takes to keep that from happening. We both know you didn't do anything wrong. They took your gun...and they knew where to find it. Everyone in this town knows where you keep those under the counter. So why was that the very last place they looked?"

"So that they would have ample opportunity to destroy every piece of furniture and upholstery that Joey hadn't?" she replied. She didn't know why the hell Silas did what he did, but she was pretty damn sure that everything the deputies had done since they'd walked into the bar had been on his orders.

"I have a bad feeling here, Lowey...if Silas wanted that

gun, it's because he knows it will match whatever slug they dig out of Joey. This would be so much easier if you had cameras in here!"

"I do," she replied. "I had them installed with the security system when I moved into the apartment upstairs. They loop every forty-eight hours." It hadn't even crossed her mind. The security cameras focused on the areas behind the bar, in front of the storeroom, and the entrance to her apartment. With Joey's shooting spree, they'd have been pointless. But if Silas or one of his minions had let himself into the bar to help themselves to her gun, they might have the proof they needed.

"What time does the loop reset?" he asked.

"At midnight," she replied.

"We've got fifteen minutes," he said. "Let's get upstairs."

Lowey followed him up the stairs to her apartment. The security feed went directly to her desktop computer. She sat down at the desk and opened up the program. Rather than try to play beat the clock, she just downloaded the file and saved it for them to review.

"Does anyone know about these cameras?" he asked.

"No. I didn't exactly advertise that I put them in. The whole point of security cameras is to not tell people where they are so then they can't avoid them."

Lowey pulled up the footage and started forwarding through the sections that she knew were clear. When they passed the point in the video where Joey had shot up the place she settled into her chair.

It took forever. Speeding up the footage, slowing it down, checking every strange blip on the screen and realizing that half of them were moths. Finally, they reached the spot where Silas entered the bar.

"Son of a bitch," Quentin said. "There he is, bold as brass."

Lowey felt sick watching it, seeing him rifling through the items behind the bar looking for the gun. When he had it in hand, he left the bar. They fast forwarded through the footage until he appeared on the screen again, placing the gun back in its normal spot.

"He killed Joey," she said slowly, stunned by what she'd just seen. "He really did, and he's going to try and burn me for it."

"Yes, he did. Email that to me and email it to my lawyer." He gave her the email addresses and then called Clayton, giving him the rundown of everything they'd found. After that, he texted the info to Ciaran.

"This stays between us and my brothers," he said. "We can't afford to let Silas know we have this until we're ready to use it. Silas is dangerous, Lowey. If he knew you had this—I don't know what he might do."

"I do," she said. "If he'd shoot Joey, he'd do that to me or worse, all without batting an eye. I don't want to go to jail, but I kinda don't want to die either."

Quentin stepped forward and pulled her into his arms. It was bad enough when he just thought Silas wanted to make her life hell, but the idea of her being in real danger, and from someone who wasn't just a fuck-up like Joey, terrified him.

"I'm not letting anything happen to you," he promised. "I'm not letting you go. Not for any reason, not ever."

"Quentin, you have gotten sucked into a huge mess... my mess. You're making all these grand statements because you're feeling heroic, but that's not who we are. I'm not a damsel in distress. I can handle this."

He laughed at that. "I know you're not, Lowey. I never thought you were. But just because you can handle it doesn't mean you should have to handle it alone. As for heroic...no. I'm not feeling heroic. I'm fucking terrified."

"What the hell are you scared of? I'm the one Silas wants dead or in prison!"

He went quiet, thinking about what he needed to say to her. "I'm scared of losing you. I can't lose anything or anyone else in my life, Lowey...but especially not you. So just let me help you with this."

"I don't understand you, Quentin. Not at all. What happened that you're suddenly this guy?"

"What guy?"

Her head fell back as she sighed with frustration. "*This* guy—the one who talks about his feelings, who admits that he actually has feelings! Where the hell did this come from?"

"It isn't that I don't have feelings. God, could this conversation make me sound like more of a pussy?" he asked. He hated these kinds of conversations. They were the primary reason that he typically avoided relationships. But avoiding one with Lowey wasn't an option. She was as necessary to him as breathing. So, if that meant he had to talk like they were on a damned episode of Dr. Phil, he would.

"Talk to me, dammit," she snapped.

"I don't let many people in. I never intended to let you in." The admission was uttered softly, but with complete conviction. It was true. He'd thought for the longest time that he could just have fun with her, just indulge his rather healthy lust for her, and then move on, like he had with so many other women in his life. But she drew him in, maybe because she was so much like him. Their backgrounds couldn't have been more different, but the way they approached the world, the way they guarded themselves, it was the same. And he'd needed to know what her secrets were, he'd needed to know why she protected herself so fiercely. That had been his first clue that she was different and that somehow, he would be different with her. "But it happened. And now that you're there, I'm not letting go, not now, not ever. I will do anything—whatever it fucking takes—to keep you safe and to keep you mine."

"So what do we do now?" she asked. "I don't know how to be this way with you, Quentin. I've spent so much time trying to pretend that this was nothing more than sex, mostly because I was terrified that any hint of emotion would send you running for the hills."

"The only running I plan to do is whatever it takes to catch you," he promised. "But first we need to get Matt Crawford out here."

"He's a Lexington cop. What's he going to do?"

"Put us in touch with someone at the state level who we can trust," he answered. "Silas is a son of a bitch, but he's not without allies. We've got to be careful with this thing."

"So how do we get in touch with him? I know he moves in your circle, but he doesn't really move in mine."

"Ciaran is sending him out...to the house. I think the best bet for us is to be where there are witnesses. Silas can't take out the whole Darcy clan without raising a shit ton of questions, but he could take out the two of us without giving it that much thought. You resisted arrest, and I interfered with the intent to harm an officer of the law...yes, it would be suspicious, but not entirely unbelievable."

She shook her head. "I miss the days of thinking Joey was the only member of the Barnes family who actually wanted to see me dead."

Nineteen

S itting in his office, feet propped up on his desk, the other deputies gone home for the night, Silas was having second thoughts. Not about the necessity of killing Joey. On that score, he was absolutely certain. But the way he'd done it had left too many loose ends. It would have been better to stage a murder-suicide—kill Lowey, set the scene to make Joey look guilty, and then stage his suicide.

He was feeling nervous and unsettled. It was a new feeling for him, and he didn't like it. Killing her *and* Quentin Darcy would be too suspicious. So, he was stuck. What to do now? What would be the best way to get out of this mess?

No sooner had the thought crossed his mind than Ciaran Darcy walked into his office. Yeah, he was stuck. Shit. That son of a bitch wouldn't be here otherwise. Silas glared at him, but the bastard just smiled at him.

"It was a nice touch," Ciaran said softly.

"What's that exactly?" Silas demanded, thought he strongly suspected that he already knew.

"Letting yourself into Lowey's bar, stealing her gun to kill your dipshit cousin, and then replacing it without anyone being the wiser...except her security cameras, of course."

The bar had a shitty security system, but he'd known about it. Cameras were something he hadn't considered she might have. Why would she bother? There was nothing in the place worth stealing. But then again, she was a woman alone, and a woman who knew all too well just how dangerous a man could be. Why wouldn't she? But he wasn't ready to admit it just yet. "You're full of shit, Darcy. And if you don't watch it, I'll be taking you to court! Those kinds of accusations aren't taken lightly."

Ciaran laughed. "Still trying to brazen it out...you may be short on brains, Barnes, but you've got balls the size of a truck!"

When he'd had Samuel Darcy in town, that would have been enough. "I've never liked the Darcys. Doing business with Samuel was a necessary evil in this town, but his high and mighty, holier-than-thou. His children? I despise the very ground they walk on...even the bastard ones like you."

The Irishman didn't appear to be the slightest bit fazed by the insult. He just smiled. "To prevent any further ugliness, I should tell you that the security footage has already been sent to several other people...you do anything to harm Harlow Tate or my brother, and you'll burn for it. It doesn't matter what you do, Barnes. You're not getting out of this."

Silas closed his eyes, let the reality of the situation sink in on him. He was done. Completely done. "Get the hell out, Darcy. Tell your brother he and his little whore are safe."

Ciaran looked at him quizzically. "You're just going to let this go quietly?"

Silas considered his options. Suicide was one. He could try to pin the murder on Harlow Tate and wind up going to prison himself. He could just put a bullet in his head and call it done. Or he could try to make a deal with the Darcys one more time. Reaching beneath his desk, he pulled out the pistol he kept there. "Lots of murders go unsolved. Joey's will be one of them...assuming you're willing to let the footage vanish."

"And if I don't?" Ciaran asked.

Silas pulled the hammer back on the revolver. "I'm not going to prison. I'll die first...and if I'm going to die, I've got nothing left to lose and nothing to stop me from taking you with me."

Ciaran nodded. "That's kind of what I thought you'd say, Silas. That's why I didn't come here alone."

Silas looked up then to see Matt Crawford and two of the state boys standing in the doorway. "Drop your weapon. Silas Barnes, you're under arrest for the murder of Joseph Barnes," one of the troopers said.

Silas did the only thing he could in that moment. He put the barrel of the gun under his chin and squeezed the trigger.

Twenty

Lowey was seated in the living room of the Darcy house, listening to Quentin explain the whole dreadful mess to his family. Annalee and Mia were sympathetic, as they would be. Clayton and Bennett were just pissed. They wanted to go beat the hell out of Silas and be done with it.

"Ciaran is handling it," Quentin replied. "He and Matt are on top of everything, and we need to stay out of it."

"Well, just look at you two!" Mia exclaimed. "Suddenly thick as thieves when you couldn't even be in a room together for more than five minutes without coming to blows."

Quentin just shrugged. "He's gone kind of above and beyond to make up for that."

At that moment, the door opened, and Matt Crawford walked into the house, Ciaran right behind him. They both looked like they'd seen better days.

"What happened?" Lowey asked.

"They're keeping your gun as evidence for the investigation, but there'll never be a trial. Silas is dead," Crawford said.

"*What*?" Lowey rose to her feet, too stunned to remain still in the wake of what they'd just told her. She couldn't quite grasp what they were telling her. "You had to kill him?"

"No," Ciaran answered reluctantly. "He killed himself. When he knew he was caught and knew that he was going to face prison for it, he put a gun under his chin and pulled the trigger."

She sank onto the sofa again as Quentin came toward her. "Are you okay?" he asked.

"I'm fine. I guess...I'm better than fine...it's over. But I just didn't expect this."

"What happens now?" He directed the question to Matt.

"Ciaran and I will have to make a formal statement about the circumstances of Silas's death. At some point, they'll probably want a deposition from you all about everything that's happened over the last two days...but then it all just goes away. It'll die down and then...nothing," Matt said.

"That seems almost anticlimactic," Lowey stated. "I had thought there would be some kind of resolution, some kind of Perry Mason-Matlock legal showdown where we all get cross examined, and then Silas gets arrested in court...I know, it was an elaborate fantasy, but that's just what I was picturing."

Ciaran nodded. "Well, that's not going to happen, and we should all be glad of it. The relationship between Silas and Samuel, the dirty money that changed hands—I know the distillery is struggling, and that could be the final nail in the coffin."

Lowey hadn't even considered it. She'd known that Quentin didn't have the kind of money most people in Fontaine thought he did, but she just thought it was because he'd poured so much into purchasing the distillery. She didn't know that the distillery itself was in trouble.

"I'm so sorry...I'm so sorry that I've put you all in the middle of this mess."

Quentin closed his arms around her and whispered next to her ear. "You didn't do this. You did nothing wrong...and as long as I'm with you, I'm right where I need to be."

"But the business—"

"Will be fine," Quentin said. "The investor is in. We'll have the capital we need to keep it going, and we'll be just fine."

He wasn't just talking about the distillery. He was talking about them. She wanted to believe that, to know that now when their lives would supposedly go back to normal that this strange intimacy that had developed between them would continue. But there was no certainty there. No trust. He'd asked for a chance to build that. And she was going to give it to him. Lowey could only pray that she wouldn't regret it.

"I just want to go home," she said. "But I don't even have one anymore. It's as shot to hell as the bar."

"Then you'll just stay with me...not at the carriage house. At my house."

There was no time for her to answer. A loud crash from the other room effectively shushed everyone. For a split second, but one that seemed to stretch on forever, everything went quiet. A pin drop would have sounded like a bomb. It was Mia who broke the spell.

"Mama," she whispered, and then took off at a dead

run for Patricia's room with everyone else following behind her.

Lowey stopped in the doorway. Patricia was on the floor, having somehow rolled out of bed. It should have been impossible. Based on what she'd always been told about Patricia's condition, it was impossible. And yet she lay there on the floor beside her hospital bed, eyes open and staring at all of them. But not sightlessly, not as if in some kind of fugue state. She was aware. She knew what was happening.

"Oh my god," Quentin whispered, the words barely audible. "Oh my god."

Clayton moved forward to lift her, but Annalee stopped him. "Don't," she said. "If she's broken a bone, moving her might make it worse. Call 9-1-1, and we'll have her taken to the hospital and checked."

Quentin still stood frozen beside her, still disbelieving and rocked to the core by what he'd seen.

"Are you okay?" she asked him.

"She really is waking up," Quentin murmured to her. "After all this time...*something* is happening."

"It certainly seems that way...we'll know more after they get her to the hospital."

Mia was making the call. And then everything became a blur. Frenzied activity followed by waiting and then EMTs rushing in.

They were in the car and on the way to the hospital before they spoke again.

Quentin was driving, and Lowey was sitting silently in the passenger seat, wondering just how much drama one person could go through in the course of a few days. Breakups, reconciliations, death threats, murder attempts, being framed by the police, and the miraculous awakening of a woman from a decade-long coma. It was all too intense.

"It's been a pretty crazy couple of days," Quentin said, mirroring her thoughts. "But that's not what we're about."

"How do we know? We don't know what it's like to be together when our lives are normal."

He grinned. "If we're together, baby, it will never be normal...I do love you, Lowey. It took walking out on you for me to figure it out. I don't want to live the rest of my life being so afraid of losing what I love that I just won't love anything."

"I love you, too. And I knew it long before you walked out...so, it's going to take me a while to get over the fact that you did. But I'm working on it."

"When I said you could stay with me...what I really meant is that I want you to move in with me."

Her mouth opened, then closed, then opened again. "Oh. That is not what I thought you meant."

"This is the real deal, Lowey. You and me. I'd ask you to marry me, but you told me once that you never wanted to get married again."

She had said that, but she was surprised he'd been paying enough attention to remember. "Never is kind of a strong word. I don't want to get married right now...I think living together to see if we can do so without killing each other might be a good place to start."

"I'll help you pack tomorrow."

It was really happening. Holy shit. "Okay. But, Quentin, if you make me regret this, I'll make what Ciaran did to you look like child's play. I mean it."

"If I make you regret it, you won't have to...and while this won't be easy, I promise that every day, I'm going to make it worth it."

Twenty-One

I t was late afternoon by the time Quentin awoke. Lowey still slept beside him. They'd spent hours at the hospital after Patricia had been taken there by ambulance. They'd consulted with specialists and with therapists and with a dozen other people it seemed. The bottom line remained that no one had any real answers. No one could tell them if her brain function had suddenly spiked or returned after ages, what had prompted any of those changes, if those changes were permanent, if there would be continued progress made. The truth was, they knew as little after the fact as they did going in.

What had become abundantly clear, thanks to the admitting physician, was that the amount of testing done previously to determine the true nature of Patricia's condition was grossly negligent. And all of that was thanks to Samuel. He'd wanted her in that state. It had made her more easily exploitable.

After it had all been said and done, Quentin had driven them to his house. All their stuff was at the carriage house and would have to be collected later, along with whatever was salvageable from Lowey's apartment. But he'd wanted her there. He'd wanted her in his bed. It was long overdue. Even though they'd both been too exhausted to do more than sleep in each other's arms, it felt right to have her there.

Rolling onto his side, Quentin stared down at her. She'd forgotten to take her makeup off, and what was left of it was pretty much smeared everywhere. Her hair was all but standing on end, but she wore nothing but a simple white T-shirt, and she was still the sexiest woman he'd ever laid eyes on.

As if sensing his gaze on her, she opened her eyes and looked up at him. "No," she said, and pulled the covers up over her head.

He laughed. "What do you mean 'no?' I haven't asked you anything!"

"I know that look, Quentin. I'm tired. I just want to sleep for a little longer."

Quentin tugged the sheets back down until she was forced to look at him. "Give me one minute to change your mind."

She glared at him, but since his hands were already stroking her legs, kneading the muscles of her calves, then her thighs, the glare became less heated. "One minute," she agreed.

He used that one minute to his advantage. Grasping the hem of her T-shirt, he pushed it upward even as he lowered himself between her thighs. With his mouth only inches from her sweet flesh, he felt her shiver with anticipation.

Parting her legs wider, opening her to him completely, he dipped his head and pressed a tender kiss to the inside of one thigh and then the other. He repeated those kisses, gradually working his way to her center. When he pressed his mouth there, letting his tongue slide between her soft folds, he found her wet and eager. Her thighs tensed beneath his hands, and her body arched beneath him.

This, he thought, was what he'd wanted all along. He'd fought it, run from it, done everything in his power to sabotage it, but it—and she—had been inevitable for him.

Lowey couldn't hold back the broken sob as his mouth moved over her. God above, he could make her crazy with just the slightest touch. It wasn't even pleasure, she realized. It was just this primal, driving need that swept her away.

The heat of his mouth, the soft but insistent sweep of his tongue on her clit, had her writhing. Then he slid two fingers inside her, filling her up and easing the ache that he'd created.

Lowey reached for him, her fingers tangling in his dark hair, but he pushed her hands away, planting them firmly on the mattress. "You move, Lowey," he whispered darkly, "And I'll stop."

"So, I'm just supposed to lie here and let you have all the fun?"

"I won't be having all the fun...I'm going to make you come again and again. I'm going to make you come until you're begging me to stop."

She didn't answer. He'd rendered her incapable of speech with another sweep of his skilled and wicked tongue. The things he did with his mouth were possibly illegal, definitely immoral, and so fucking amazing, she thought she'd die from the pleasure of it. But she didn't reach for him again. She gripped the bedclothes bunched beneath her fingers and lay there, letting him torture her with his mouth.

He kept her there, hovering on the brink of release. Every time she would get close, he would move away or change speed or pressure. He was tormenting her, and they both knew it.

"Damn you," she whispered brokenly.

"Do you want to come, Harlow?"

He sounded so calm, so reasonable, as if he were asking her if she wanted a cup of coffee. "You're killing me!"

"If you want it, all you have to do is ask," he said, his teeth grazing her inner thigh.

"Make me come."

"Please," he corrected.

"Make me come, please," she said, but the words were about as far from subservient as possible, as they were uttered between clenched teeth. But they did the trick. He lowered his mouth to her once more. His touch was different—more direct, more insistent, and it rocked her straight to her soul.

Lowey closed her eyes as the tension built again, climbing higher than before. She screamed when it broke, sobbing as the waves of pleasure crashed within her.

She was still shaking with her orgasm, her body trembling from the force of it when he rose above her. He yanked her T-shirt off entirely, leaving her completely naked before him. But as he moved between her thighs, Lowey decided she had other plans for him. She pressed her hands against his chest, halting him right where he was.

"I get to be in charge now," she stated. "On your back, Darcy. I've got plans for you."

A wicked grin flashed across his lips just before he kissed her senseless. But then he did as she asked, rolling onto his back and bringing her with him. Lowey rose onto her knees, straddling him with ease. Lifting herself up slightly, she closed her fingers around him and guided him to her entrance. But with just the tip inside her, she stopped. It was torture for her, but it was also torture for him, and she had a little payback to get.

"Are you gonna stop there? Really?" he asked.

She moved her hips, sinking down just a bit before retreating again. "Maybe. Just the tip...isn't that what all the boys ask for?"

His gripped her hips tightly, his fingers digging into the soft flesh there. "I'm not a boy, now am I?"

Truer words had never been spoken, she thought. He was all man. Infuriating and maddening, but so damn sexy she couldn't resist him. Even as she had the thought, he lifted his own hips off the bed, surging upward, filling her so completely that any thoughts of payback faded to nothing. In fact, she lost the ability to think it all. Her world reduced to the points of contact between their bodies as she took him even deeper.

Lowey circled her hips, riding him at a slow, easy pace. But there was nothing easy about it. The sensation of having him inside her, of his hands on her body, left her wrecked. She was sobbing, crying out as he surged into her again. Every thrust brought her closer to that edge until, finally, she tumbled over it again. He was there with her, holding her tight as he pressed deep one last time.

Lying there together, their limbs tangled, sweat drying on their bodies, Lowey sighed contentedly. "Okay, so that was totally worth letting you be in charge."

He laughed softly as he stroked her back in soft lazy circles with the pad of his thumb. "Was I in charge? Seems to me you turned that table and then set it on fire."

She smiled, her face pressed against his chest. "Maybe. But are you complaining?"

"No...never."

"So what happens now?"

"Sleep?"

She smacked his chest. "That's not what I meant, and you know it. You asked me to move in here...but are you sure?"

He rolled her onto her back and then kissed her soundly. "Yes, I'm sure. I wouldn't have said it otherwise."

"I want this to work," she said. "I don't want either of us to regret it."

He sighed then, pressed his forehead to hers while his hands tangled in her hair. "The only thing I'm ever going to regret is the time I wasted...I wasn't going to say anything to you about this. I know it's too soon for you. Hell, it's too soon for me. But this is going to be forever, Lowey. And as soon as I can put a ring on your finger without people acting like we're fucking nuts, I'm going to."

"You do realize three days ago we weren't even speaking to one another?"

"It's been an action packed three days...if you let me go back to sleep for an hour or two, it'll be even more action packed when I wake up."

"Let's just hold off on talking about marriage...not because I don't want it, but because that's not what you or your family needs to focus on right now. When things are more certain with Patricia, then we'll talk about it again," she said.

"Deal," he said. "Now, go to sleep. 'Cause you're gonna need it."

Epilogue

Quentin carried the bag of ice out to the deck as Bennett fired up the grill. It was a strange thing still to see any member of the Hayes family with the run of the place. It was stranger still to see them all gathered there on the back lawn. Hayes and Darcy alike, they were all present and accounted for. Bennett was there, along with his formerly ne'er do well cousin, Carter. It seemed reform was going around, because Josie Marcum-Hayes had him walking the straight and narrow. Savannah was there as well, and even Emmitt, the hermit, had been dragged into civilization for the day. They made a motley bunch to be sure.

Sitting in her wheelchair on the porch, Patricia was looking out on all of them. She'd come so far but still seemed to be struggling to fit back into the world after being lost to it for so long. After he dumped the ice in the chest to chill the drinks, Quentin walked over and squatted down beside her.

"Bet this is something you never expected to see," he

said, gesturing toward the wary looking Hayes clan all gathered together.

"Not expected. Hoped," she said. Her words were still halting, slow—every one of them chosen and enunciated with care. Walking was coming back slower than talking, but that, according to the doctors and therapists, was to be expected. Even with all that Mia and the others had done to help her maintain range of motion, her muscles had atrophied.

"She's happy," Quentin said, looking at his sister who was glowing with it. She stood next to Lowey and Annalee as they watched Emma Grace dancing around with abandon.

"You are, too," Patricia said knowingly.

He ducked his head and grinned. "Yes, I am. I told Lowey that we wouldn't bring up marriage again until things with you were more settled. How settled do you feel, Mama?"

"I love weddings," Patricia answered with a smile. It was a little crooked, the right side of her face still partially paralyzed. But that smile meant more to him than the world.

Quentin rose and leaned over to kiss her cheek. "Good. 'Cause I'm giving her Grandma's ring."

"Where did you get it?" Patricia demanded.

"You told me when I was sixteen that it was mine to give to whatever girl I wanted...so, on Thanksgiving, after Ciaran beat the pis—crap out of me, and all I could think about was Lowey, I went up to your room and got it," he confessed.

"Then go give it to her and stop talking my ear off!"

"Tonight. I'm not going to put her on the spot in front of everyone. She might say no just to spite me." He didn't really think she'd turn him down, but there was just enough fear in him to make him think asking in private was the best way to preserve his pride.

"Go. Go and get her. Take her inside and ask that girl, Quentin!" Patricia urged. "There's nothing worse than wasted time!"

She'd know, he thought sadly. Impulsively, he hugged her again. "I missed you, Mama. I missed you every day."

She touched his face, patting it the same way she had when he was a little boy. "I was always here," she said and tapped the center of his forehead with her finger.

"My conscience," he added with a grin.

She shrugged. "Maybe."

Quentin left her then and made his way over to where Lowey stood. Annalee and Mia simply drifted away, as if sensing that he wanted privacy.

"I need to talk to you," he whispered against her ear.

"Quentin Darcy, if you're going to dump me here in the middle of your family gathering—"

He bit her ear, his teeth nipping at the soft shell of it just a bit less than gently. "Shut up, Lowey."

"Don't tell me to shu—"

He pulled the ring box from his pocket and pressed it into her palm. She didn't exactly stop talking as much as the words simply faded into unintelligible gibberish. When she'd collected herself, even though her hands still trembled in his, she asked, "What is this?"

"What does it look like? It's an engagement ring."

"But your mother—"

"Is looking forward to attending a wedding. She missed Clayton's, and for whatever reason, Bennett and Mia don't seem to be in any hurry...so, marry me and make her a happy woman," he urged.

Lowey glared at him. "Really? We're getting married for your mama's sake?"

He grinned. "It might be just a little bit for my benefit too. Marry me, Harlow Tate...I'd ask you to make an honest man of me, but frankly, I don't think it's possible."

"You're honest. You're just an asshole," she snarked. "But I kinda like that about you, so I guess I'm saying yes."

Quentin kissed her then and pried the box from her hand long enough to take the ring out of it and slip it on her finger. "No regrets, Lowey. Not now and not ever."

"Just one...you should have asked me before you knocked me up."

Quentin dropped his head onto her shoulder and laughed aloud in surprised delight. "You've been saving that bit of info just to one-up me, haven't you?"

"Yes. I absolutely have."

"It worked," he admitted. "I love you, Lowey. And I'm going to spend the rest of my life proving it to you and whatever hellion offspring we manage to produce."

"I'm going to hold you to that, hotshot." She kissed him then, so sweetly that they both just ignored the retching sounds that came from Emma Grace the catcalls from everyone else.

From the porch, Patricia surveyed her children. It had been a long journey back to them. She'd never tell them the truth, that for ten long and hellish years she'd lain in that hospital bed hearing everything that happened around her. She'd known of their tears and heartbreaks, of their fights and victories. But she'd been powerless to do anything for them. And yet, somehow, they'd triumphed without her.

They'd succeeded in life even when she hadn't been able to guide them and help them. It gratified on one level but stung on another. They didn't need her, not really. Oh, she knew they were happy to have her among them again, but it wasn't the same. Their relationships would never be the same. They'd been on the other side of the fence, taking care of her. It would always be different now.

As she let her gaze wander over them, she noted the protective hand Quentin had placed on Lowey's belly. She'd had her suspicions about that. While Lowey hadn't said anything, she'd noted how peaked she looked in the mornings lately.

"Gramma, they're all just gross!"

Patricia smiled as Emma Grace flopped down beside her on the porch. "Kissing only seems gross now. You'll change your mind soon enough." She'd have another grandchild soon, one she could know and spoil from birth, but the precious angel sitting beside her, who'd read her stories and chattered endlessly to her while she'd been trapped in her own body, that child would always be special to her.

"Never," her granddaughter vowed.

Patricia realized then that while her children might not need her, this little girl did. And the others would too. Quentin's and Lowey's first and one day, Bennett and Mia would make beautiful babies for her to spoil. Grandchildren would always need their grandparents, she thought.

Bonus Material

THE FIRST TIME

Quentin Darcy rolled into The Kicking Mule ten minutes before closing, and he did it the same way he did everything else—like it was his God-given right. The place was empty except for her and now him. Standing behind her bar, polishing glasses that had seen better days and wondering if there was enough cash in the till to cover the cost of even keeping the place open that night, he was definitely the bright spot of her night.

Cocky and with every right to be, he walked in like he owned the place. He was so damned sexy that it hurt just to look at him. Crisp, button-down shirt with the cuffs rolled back and well-tailored pants that displayed a finely sculpted ass, he had clearly just left the distillery. They'd been dancing around one another for weeks. He'd come into the bar a few times. They'd run into one another in town a time or two. A little harmless flirting, or at least that's what she'd thought initially. Then he'd texted her. She hadn't asked how he got her number. He was a Darcy, after all. If they wanted something, they got it. Every damn one of them.

Lowey kept her gaze locked on him as he approached the bar and took a seat on one of the battered and cracked vinyl barstools.

"Can I get a beer?"

"I don't know if we have anything on tap fancy enough for you," she said. Immediately, she regretted it. Just because she was well too aware of the difference in their social standing was no reason to comment on it. That just gave him the upper hand.

But he smiled. "Whatever you've got is fine," he said.

Lowey grabbed one of the mugs and pulled the beer. The head on it was perfect. So the bar was a shithole, that didn't mean she had to be a shitty bartender.

He glanced at the mug and smiled. "I'm impressed."

"You ought to be," she shot back.

He looked around the bar. "You know, considering this is the only place in or around Fontaine that serves alcohol, I thought it'd be busier."

"Even drunks take a night off every now and then," she said. "It's summertime, Mr. Darcy. Where people prefer to do their drinking on the creek bank while they fish."

"And how do you like to spend your summer nights?"

She knew precisely how she wanted to spend her night. It involved her legs wrapped around him and his hands on her body. But she wouldn't say it. She wouldn't give him the satisfaction. "You're asking very personal questions, Quentin Darcy."

"I want to get very personal, Harlow Tate," he replied, and his voice was so rich and deep it shivered straight through her.

There was something in the way he said her name that told her they were no longer talking about just having drinks or making idle chatter. This was pointed and laden with tension. It hit her instantly, the healthy dose of lust that arced through her and made her clench her thighs together with anticipation.

"What are you really doing here, Quentin? If you'd just wanted a drink, you've got a better stock than anyone else in this town."

"We've been playing this game for a while now, Lowey. But sidelong glances and a lot of hot fantasies will only take a man so far."

"And what makes you think I'm interested in that?" she demanded.

"I saw you," he said. "You were walking down Main Street, and I saw you..."

"And that's why you're here? Because you saw me? They call that stalking, Mr. Darcy," she fired back.

"And you saw me," he continued, as if she hadn't accused him of being a creeper. "It was written on your face, Harlow, plain as day. You want me as bad as I want you."

"I want lots of things that aren't good for me...chocolate, whiskey! You're still a stalker," she said, but there was no real heat in it.

He grinned as he set his glass down on the bar. "It's only stalking if you don't want me to be here. Should I go, Lowey? Or should I stay?"

Stay. It was an immediate and knee-jerk response. The way he looked at her—no man had looked at her like that in a long time, if ever, and certainly not one like him. Quentin Darcy was not a commitment kind of guy. It was stamped all over him, but as far as she knew, he wasn't a player either. He wasn't the type to make promises and break them. He just didn't make them at all.

"What are you really after, Darcy?" she asked.

"I don't want to be alone tonight, Harlow...and I have

the feeling you don't either. What's the harm in us keeping each other company?"

"You could talk the devil into turning up the heat," she replied.

"Then close up early," he suggested. "Take me upstairs and let me convince you of just how hot it needs to be."

Had there ever been a better offer? No, she thought. Not even once. "Lock the door," she said.

A Look at On the Fence

THREE RIVERS TREVORS RANCH BOOK ONE
BY J.S. WOOD

He thought pushing her away would keep her safe. Now he's back, and he's not leaving without her.

CT Trevors made the biggest mistake of his life when he walked away from Dani West, thinking he was saving her from heartbreak. But when her cousin reaches out, saying Dani needs help with a horse that's suddenly gone skittish, CT sees his chance—a second chance to make things right.

Dani doesn't want his help. She's still smarting from the way he ended things, and the last thing she needs is CT stirring up old feelings. But she knows he's the only trainer for miles who can get her back in the ring.

As they work side by side, secrets from her past trainer come to light, and old wounds start to heal. Dani says they're just working together. CT says he's winning her heart back. She insists she's done with him for good.

But CT's ready to fight for her this time—even if it scares him to death.

AVAILABLE NOW

Sweet, sassy, southern, small town romance.

Chasity Bowlin is a *USA Today* bestselling author of numerous romance novels. She resides in central Kentucky with her husband, their charming son, and a lively menagerie of animals. A passionate traveler, Chasity enjoys weaving glimpses of her real-life adventures into her stories. As an avid Anglophile, she adores all things British, with a particular love for the Regency era.

Born and raised in Tennessee, Chasity spent much of her childhood with her doting grandparents, where soap operas and back-to-back episodes of Scooby-Doo were part of her daily routine. Her path to becoming a romance novelist was perhaps inevitable—her Barbie dolls didn't just cruise in pink convertibles; they traveled through time, hosted extravagant dinner parties, and one even had an evil twin locked in the attic.

www.chasitybowlin.com